CRIME FROM ANOTHER TIME

STORIES OF MYSTERY AND SUSPENSE

DAVID H. HENDRICKSON

ꟼP
Pestachi
Publishing

Springtime in Paris had always been magical for Monique Bardet and for so many reasons. Cherry blossoms at the Notre Dame Cathedral. The Luxembourg gardens in full bloom. Outdoor cafés filled with happy couples, the smells of freshly brewed coffee and *croissants* wafting from their canopied tables. Walking along the Seine, crisp gusts of air lifting her flowing blonde hair off her slender shoulders as if each strand was but a feather.

But there was nothing magical about springtime in Paris now. Nor had there been for the last four years since German troops marched into the city after the traitor Philippe Pétain surrendered the country under the pretext of an armistice and its illusion of country still partially free.

Now, German soldiers and officials sat at the café tables. German plays had corrupted the *Théâtre des Champs-Élysées,* and the Berlin Philharmonic had taken its seats at the *Opéra Garnier* while the red Nazi flags with their loathsome swastikas, black against a circle of white, flew outside. Framed against the *Arc de Triomphe*, German tanks and goose-stepping soldiers had paraded down the *Champs-Élysées.*

Arc de Triomphe? More like *Arc de Défaite.*

PRAISE FOR DAVID H. HENDRICKSON

Crime From Another Time
Stories of Mystery and Suspense

"When the Sun Goes Down," originally appeared in *Pulphouse Fiction Magazine*, Issue #13, edited by Dean Wesley Smith, WMG Publishing, Inc., August, 2021

"Devil in Disguise," originally appeared in *More Groovy Gumshoes: Private Eyes in the Psychedelic Sixties*, edited by Michael Bracken, Down & Out Books, April, 2023

"*Gacaca*" originally appeared in *Mystery, Crime, and Mayhem: Passionate Crimes*, edited by Leah Cutter, Knotted Row Press, May, 2021

"Huram's Temple," originally appeared in *Ellery Queen's Mystery Magazine,* edited by Janet Hutchings, March/April, 2015

"Housewarming Gift," originally appeared in *Mystery, Crime, and Mayhem: Sins of the Father*, edited by Leah Cutter, Knotted Row Press, October, 2020

"Squirrel and Worm," originally appeared in *Thrill Ride – the Magazine: Unlikely Partners*, edited by M.L. Buchman, Buchman Bookworks, Inc., June, 2023

ISBN-13: 978-1-948134-21-7

CONTENTS

To John D. MacDonald
and
Robert B. Parker,
whose novels were my earliest
influences in this genre.

INTRODUCTION

Admittedly, writing mystery and suspense stories from another era poses difficulties not found when sticking to the here and now. Considerable effort must be spent establishing an unfamiliar setting. How much research is too much? And God forbid you get an important detail wrong. Off with the offending writer's head!

All true, but writing such stories also opens up great opportunities. Tales that wouldn't make sense in modern America become not just possible but exciting and new. Exploring different cultures and themes becomes great fun. And all that fun applies not just to the writer but to the reader too.

A win-win.

These stories range from as recent as thirty years ago (but in a very different culture) to the sixties to World War 2 France to ancient times. I hope you have as good a time reading them as I did writing them.

WHEN THE SUN
GOES DOWN

INTRODUCTION TO WHEN THE SUN GOES DOWN

I love cold cases. Both writing and reading them. The more difficult, the better. But a sixty-five-year-old case? Before DNA? With no forensic evidence at all?

That ain't cold. That's impossible.

I wrote "When the Sun Goes Down" for an anthology themed on "secrets." As it turned out, another writer had also submitted a story that dealt with racial issues. Totally different stories. *Totally*. Neither of us had lazily opted for the kind of "low-hanging fruit" that often results in duplication.

Even so, we were still "competing" for one slot. The editor's vision for her anthology did not allow for two stories on that topic, no matter how much she liked them both. What worked against "When the Sun Goes Down" was that it was considerably longer than the other, and the editor was fighting firm word count limitations established by the publisher. As a result, she chose the shorter story.

That happens. It's the risk that accompanies higher

word counts. Invariably, editors receive more stories they like, or even love, than they can fit in their anthology. So they'll pick two 4,500-word stories over a single 9,000-worder. Completely understandable. I'm sure that over the years some of my 3,000- and 4,000-word stories have enjoyed the other side of that coin.

No matter what, you have to write the story you believe in, then deal with the consequences. Otherwise, what's the point? If there's a firm word count limitation, you might be able to trim it to get under the ceiling while staying true to your vision. If not, you submit that tale elsewhere and write another one that meets the requirement. In this case, though, there was no word count limitation that I'd exceeded. My disadvantage only came to light after the fact.

Too late to change anything.

Even so, I wouldn't have changed a word. I'd told the tale I wanted to tell. That's all you can do, then move on.

Fortunately, "When the Sun Goes Down" wasn't left out in the cold for long. Dean Wesley Smith deemed the story "flat wonderful" and published it in lucky issue number 13 of *Pulphouse Fiction Magazine*.

WHEN THE SUN GOES DOWN

Latisha Watkins was making the rounds at her cousin's wedding reception, catching up with relatives and old friends, some of whom she hadn't seen since leaving Tulsa for Boston ten years earlier. She'd gotten her Bachelor's degree in Criminal Justice and stayed up north, becoming first a street cop and then a detective in a gritty, downtrodden city north of Boston that had no shortage of crime. She'd returned a few times, but this was her first extended vacation back here since her childhood. The timing left a lot to be desired—who left Boston for Oklahoma in July instead of January?—but it was great to see everyone again anyway.

The band had taken a break, which had also given Latisha a break from all the dances with old boyfriends and total strangers. She hadn't overdone it with her black dress. Not cut too low, since she didn't have that much to show anyway. Not too short either; she certainly could have shown off her sleek brown legs to better advantage. But there was no hiding her attractive figure, and the men had apparently noticed that, or perhaps the pleasing complexion of her dark brown face, or her bright smile, or simply that she was having a good time moving about the dance floor.

But it had been a well-timed break by the band. The air was filled with the smells of colognes and perfumes, and of the tomato sauce, beef, and chicken from the main course. The buzz of conversation filled the air, punctuated by silverware clinking on plates by those still eating the, by all accounts, sinfully delicious caramel cheesecake topped with strawberries and whipped cream.

Too sinful for Latisha's taste. It was the kind of dessert you gained five pounds just looking at. So she began to move from one circular table to another, each with its white lace tablecloth, place settings and wine glasses, and ornate flower arrangement at the center. In due time she got to her Grandma June, perched near the rear of the hall, table nineteen out of twenty, all but three of the other nine at her table off to the bar or restroom or circulating just like Latisha.

She sat in the seat to her grandmother's left and smiled. It wasn't forced. She couldn't help but smile when she was around the woman. Grandma June had aged considerably since they'd last seen each other. She was thin now almost to the point of being skeletal, her white flowered dress hanging limply off her shoulders. A gust of wind might carry her away, or if it knocked her down, it would shatter every bone in her fragile body. But Latisha thought she still saw the old spark in her grandma's eyes.

"Grandma June, you're looking great!" Latisha lied.

Grandma June gave her a shooing away gesture. "I'm getting awfully close to ninety years old. My wrinkles have wrinkles. I can't get from this table to the next one without this damned walker here behind me." She pointed her thumb over her right shoulder to the walker parked behind the empty seat to her right. "How great is that?" But she followed her words with a playful wink. Grandma June hadn't lost her touch.

"I hope I'm doing that great at ninety!" Latisha said.

"I didn't say I was ninety, child! I'm not even eighty-nine. Not even eighty-eight. I just said I was awfully close... to *the big nine-oh-shit*!"

Latisha laughed. "It's great to see you again."

After more pleasantries, Grandma June said, "I've got a favor to ask."

Grandma June had always been one of her favorites, so Latisha said, "Sure."

"A big one."

"Okay."

"A really big one."

"What?" Latisha asked, her carefully trimmed thin eyebrows raised, a sense of foreboding rising.

"I hear you're a big shot detective up there in Boston."

"I'm a detective north of Boston," Latisha said. "But I'm no big shot."

"You any good?"

Latisha chuckled ruefully. The question reminded her of her crusty old bastard of a partner up north who'd speculated aloud as soon as they were paired that she must have gotten her bump to detective because "you got brown skin and you got tits." It was a mistake he made only once, but the unstated doubts had remained until two months ago when Latisha solved a high-profile murder, no thanks to him.

"You doubt me, Grandma?" Latisha asked, her head cocked.

"Hell no, I just wanted to hear you brag," Grandma June said, and they both laughed.

"To use a phrase my favorite grandma always used to say," Latisha said, a twinkle in her brown eyes, "I am... the cat's meow."

They laughed some more, Grandma June slapping the table with joy. Yeah, Grandma June still had it. She might be confined to her walker, but that clever mind of hers was still sharp as a tack.

"So what can I do for you?" Latisha asked.

"I saw on the TV some hot shot detectives solving something they called a cold case," Grandma June said. "You know, a case that's decades old and everyone has forgotten it?"

Latisha smiled. She didn't exactly need Grandma June to explain what a cold case is. "I know the term."

"Well I got thinking about my beautiful, intelligent hot shot detective of a granddaughter, and I got thinking that I had a cold case for her."

Latisha's smile froze. She'd come down here on vacation, not to hear about cold cases, much less have one dropped into her lap by a grandmother she'd never been able to say no to.

"I'm sorry. I shouldn't have said a thing," Grandma June said. "I can see it in your face. You don't even want to hear about it. And I don't blame you one bit. No, not one bit. It was inconsiderable for me to even mention it. I should be ashamed of myself."

"Tell me," Latisha said, feeling guilty herself now.

"No, I was just being a selfish old woman. Run along now." Grandma June gave her a shooing away gesture. "Looks like the tongues of some of those men you danced with are about to fall out of their mouths, they panting so hard for you."

"Grandma June, if you don't tell me about this cold case right this instant, you will be condemning me to a wasted life of hopelessness and misery."

Grandma June smiled knowingly. "That's my girl."

And they were laughing again.

Grandma June said, "Since you're forcing me to tell you—"

"I am. I am."

"Okay, then."

Grandma June's smile disappeared. Her face turned hard and cold as stone. The joy that had been dancing in her eyes was gone, replaced by a sad, faraway look. She took in a deep breath and sighed.

"Back in 1955, I was married to a man named Floyd Jackson. A good man, handsome and kind. Short, but with broad shoulders, he was. A hard worker. He was my first husband. We never had children cause we was only married a short time.

"Your grandfather John, God rest his soul, came later, and John had a bit of a jealous streak, not that I gave him no reason. So he didn't want to hear no mention of Floyd, no matter what had happened to him. It was as if Floyd had never existed, which wasn't fair, but that's the way it was back then. If your man said something, you did it. If he told you never to mention a name again, you didn't. People might have talked about Floyd, but not in John's presence."

Latisha nodded. She had heard a few things whispered, but wasn't sure where fact ended and fiction began. Lies were more easily whispered than truths.

"We lived in an all-black town called Langston. I worked there, but Floyd worked at a farm a few miles away on the edge of a town called Charlton. Walked those miles there and back each day without complaint, always a smile. A hard worker. Probably about five thousand people there in Charlton, all white except for the black men and women like Floyd who went there to work during the day and came home at night. They didn't count in no census or population total.

"Well, one night, he didn't come home. Simple as that. A Wednesday night I remember clear as if it was yesterday. Everything had been fine the day before. No worries. No concerns. Other than how we was going to pay the rent, of course, and if we could ever afford a fan to get some relief from the heat that just baked the sweat to your bones, but wasn't nothing new about that. Just happened out of the blue. He didn't come home.

"I was frantic. I knew the others who went into Charlton. Seventeen in all, fourteen men, including Floyd, and three women. They'd walk together sometimes, if they was leaving at the same time, but they all worked at different farms and businesses so it wasn't very practical on the way home unless they happened to come upon each other. Wasn't like there was some place in that town where black people could socialize before all going home together. It was 'Negro, get... out... of... town.'

"Well I ran up and down the streets of Langston— back in those days, I could run like the wind, not like now —and I knocked on all the doors of those who worked in Charlton, but none of them knew a thing. Said they never saw Floyd. Thought that like any other day, he was either ahead of them on the road back home or behind. No one thought too much about it until I came knocking, bawling my eyes out, knowing something was wrong.

"The next evening, two of those men who worked in Charlton returned with Floyd's body. It was wrapped in sheets. They told me not to look, but I couldn't help myself. It was the most awful thing I ever saw."

Grandma June stared off into the distance and shook her head.

"The Klan got him. That handsome face wasn't handsome no more. They beat his strong body into an ugly pulp. They didn't lynch him, but they might as well have. Worst thing I ever saw."

"I'm so sorry," Latisha said, a lump in her throat.

"The next day, I got leave from my work, and went to that farm where Floyd worked. I asked them what they had done to my man. What had he done to deserve that? But they had been as shocked as me. They had liked Floyd. He worked hard for them and gave them no trouble.

"Last they saw him that day was in the middle of the afternoon, but after that he got all his work done, getting feed into the stalls, giving the cows their evening milking, and shoeing two of the horses. They never actually saw him leave, but that wasn't nothing strange. He was just supposed to finish his work, close up the barn, and head home. They didn't know nothing was wrong until he didn't show up the next morning.

"Wasn't until the next Monday, five days after he was killed, that the men who worked in Charlton came back with what the Klan was saying Floyd done. They was told my Floyd, who wouldn't hurt a fly, attempted to rape a woman. A white woman, of course. They wouldn't care if it was one of us. No name. Just a white woman.

"But it was a lie. Floyd would never do that. I know my Floyd. He wasn't that kind of man. He would never have done anything like that. Not to any woman, white or black. He wouldn't even *look* at a white woman. He was no fool. This was Oklahoma. He knew the rules."

Latisha realized she'd been holding her breath. "How awful!" It was a stupid thing to say that she regretted as soon as the words were out of her mouth. Of course it was awful. But what else could she say?

"Nowadays, most everyone has forgotten about my Floyd," Grandma June said. "And those who do remember his name wonder if it all was true. They think my Floyd could really have done such an awful thing. It's sad how easily some people will believe the worst of lies. Now, you say the name Floyd Jackson and you either get a blank stare, never heard of him, or the vague recollection of a man who attacked a white woman and got beaten to death for it."

Silence hung in the air between Latisha and Grandma June even as all about them conversation buzzed. Grandma June placed a cold and bony hand on Latisha's.

"I know it's been a lot of years, but could you find out what really happened? Can you clear my Floyd's good name so when people hear it, the awful thing they think about is what was done to him and the injustice of it, and not what awful thing he might have done to deserve it?"

Latisha swallowed hard. This would be impossible. Almost everyone involved was likely dead or mentally compromised. Or would have no intention of exposing the truth. She wasn't even a cold case detective, and this was the coldest of cold cases. No DNA or other forensic evidence. No leads. Not even any jurisdiction.

Nothing.

"It'll take a miracle."

Grandma June nodded and smiled. "Then I'll pray for a miracle."

LATISHA DECIDED to give it a day. For Grandma June. And maybe, Latisha thought, for herself, too. Because this kind of thing was important. She'd be down here for a week. One day of lost vacation time wouldn't kill her. Although she suspected she'd soon get sucked into a second day and then a third and who knew how much longer.

Likely for nothing.

At nine the next morning, she parked her Hyundai rental in front of the Charlton police station in a yellow-lined space next to an empty cruiser on her right, leaving the car running for the A/C. The building, made of old bricks now dirty and crumbling, housed the post office on the right and the police station on the left. It was on Main Street, half a mile from the center of town.

According to demographic information Latisha had looked up online, Charlton was no longer entirely white, although it was close, over ninety-five percent, broken up by a smattering of Hispanics, Native Americans, and yes, even African Americans. Nonetheless, every face she saw on her drive into town had been a white one.

She figured she'd start with the police chief. It never hurt for a cop to check in with her local counterpart as a matter of professional courtesy, even if there was a chance the relationship could turn adversarial. And in an ideal world, there'd even be a file on the case online, although the likelihood of that was admittedly right up there with Santa Claus being real and Jimmy Hoffa still living and breathing. Even so, it was the natural place to start.

She scanned again Grandma June's two sets of hand-written notes to at least remind herself of the names. The first set, comprised of three pages stapled together in the upper left hand corner, listed all the black laborers who had gone into Charlton back in 1955. Sixteen, other than Floyd Jackson, of course, from Langston, and fourteen from other nearby predominantly black communities. Unfortunately, every single man and woman had passed away except for Jerome Hightower and Mildred Reynolds, both of whom were in advanced stages of Alzheimer's and would be of no help.

Grandma June had done that much checking herself,

and had even called as many of those workers' relatives as she could track down, listing all their phone numbers and addresses, but none of them knew a thing about Floyd Jackson. It was three pages of dead ends.

"You need to talk to the white people in that town," Grandma June had said. "The old Klan members that are still around. That's something I haven't been able to do."

But where to start? She'd said that any white adult male in Charlton back then could have been a Klan member, and in fact it might have been an expected rite of passage to join upon entering adulthood, no different than getting a driver's license. So any adult white male alive in 1955 in a town of five thousand was a suspect.

Great. Even on duty with all the normal resources available to a detective, she'd be lucky to track down the leads in a month. As a private citizen, a week was impossible.

Fortunately, Grandma June had another handwritten list she'd prepared, this one with the names of all the town leaders and most prominent men back in 1955, as best as she'd been able to reconstruct. The mayor, councilmen, school committee members, chief of police, clergymen, and leading businessmen. Thirty-four names in all. Beside all but three names, printed in neat block letters, was the word GONE, sometimes with an out-of-state address next to it, or the word DEAD. Beside the other three names, however, were their last known phone number and address.

Grandma June sure was no stereotypical octogenarian, barely able to handle e-mail and susceptible to even the most basic of scams. She was a wily user of the Internet, and she'd done her homework. As soon as Latisha was finished with the police chief, she'd check out the three names. All they represented was the identity of former community leaders who were apparently still alive. There was no confirmation that they'd ever been members of the Klan, much less involved in Floyd Jackson's murder. Latisha could only hope that that was the case because finding a peon from the Klan all those years ago would be like finding a needle in the proverbial haystack.

Latisha turned off the ignition and bounded up the concrete steps to the front door, the heat slamming into her like a wall. She wore beige slacks, matching sandals, and a light yellow, flowered blouse. She stepped to a waist-high wooden counter that ran from one dark blue-colored wall to the other, fifty feet or so in all. A middle-aged woman in a tan skirt and blouse sat at a desk behind the counter, working on a computer. She looked up, did a double-take, pursed her lips, and said, "One minute."

Behind her were three walled-in offices, the upper half of their front walls all glass, the center office as large as the other two combined. Black lettering on the center door read: Police Chief on one line and Stephen J. Thompson on the next. Gray metal filing cabinets lined both side walls.

In due time, the woman stepped to the counter, a cloud of overpowering jasmine perfume moving with her.

"May I help you?"

"My name is Latisha Watkins. I'm a detective from the

Boston area in town on personal business." She flashed her badge. "I'd like to speak to the chief, if I may."

The woman's eyebrows had shot up at the word "detective." A shocked look remained on her face.

"Is there a problem?" she asked.

"No, I'd just like to speak to the chief."

The woman stood frozen for a moment. Finally, she rallied and asked, "May I ask what this is about?"

Latisha felt like answering *none of your fucking business*, but instead smiled graciously and said, "An old case. It doesn't involve him, but I thought there was a remote chance he might have some information."

A minute later, Chief Thompson stood at the office door and waved her inside. He was heavy-set, a shade under six feet tall and at least 230 pounds, maybe even pushing 250, the shirt buttons of his uniform close to popping when he turned. He was bald and with a florid complexion.

Standing beside his desk as she entered, he asked, "Is there a problem, Miss..."

"Ms. Watkins. Latisha Watkins." She offered her hand and he shook it, squeezing it a little too hard, apparently to make clear who had testosterone pumping in his blood and two big balls in his shorts and who was lacking both. It was a petty, macho show of strength she'd seen so many times, it only barely registered.

"I'm not here on official business," Latisha said, after they both sat down, her in a straight-backed, gray metal padded chair on the other side of the desk from the chief. Two sets of green hanging folders sat on opposite sides of the desktop along with a white coffee cup with the words

"Because I'm the chief!" in big black letters. The smell of the coffee filled the air. In the office off to their right, an air conditioner noisily rattled.

"Then why are you here?" Thompson asked, looking annoyed, the unstated thought being, *why the hell are you bothering me*?

"I'm doing an investigation on my own time," Latisha said. "I wanted to inform you. As a matter of professional courtesy. And also, although it's an extreme long shot, see if you have any information that might help."

Thompson frowned. "What sort of investigation?"

"You might say this is the coldest of cold cases. It goes back to 1955."

"1955! That's—" He paused, apparently doing the arithmetic in his head, having to do it twice to make sure he got it right. "That's over sixty-five years ago!"

Latisha felt the urge to pat his bald white head and say, "Good boy! And you did it all without using your fingers!" Instead, she said, "As I said, I know it's a long shot—"

"So it's a murder case," Thompson said, resting both beefy, black-haired forearms on the desktop. "That's the only crime without a statute of limitations in this state. Anything else and you're wasting your time. If this is a 'MeToo' crusade, you're wasting your time. Statute of limitations on rape is seven years."

While inside she burned, Latisha replied, "It's a murder case."

"So you're looking to reopen a murder case over sixty-five years old. About two thousand miles out of your jurisdiction up there in *Ass*-achusetts," he said, leaving out the M in the state so he could emphasize the *ass*.

The man needed a good slap in the face, Latisha thought, but she guessed, just took a wild-ass guess, that doing so would be counterproductive.

"I want to clear a man's name," Latisha said.

Chief Thompson's eyebrows shot up. "A man wrongfully convicted? Of murder?"

"No, the victim."

Thompson flinched. "I'm not understanding you."

"An African American," Latisha said, and wasn't surprised to see Thompson lean back in his chair, suddenly less interested. "A black man beaten to death for no apparent reason and left on the outskirts of town so the crows could peck out his eyeballs. Man by the name of Floyd Jackson."

Thompson's body stiffened. Recognition flashed in his eyes. His intake of a breath halted for a split second.

Then the telltale signs were all gone, replaced by a look of practiced calm and disinterest.

"The Klan did it, of course" Latisha said, looking for additional signs that the police chief knew every last detail about what she was saying, that he didn't just recognize the name Floyd Jackson but he knew the whole story. But Thompson wasn't showing anything now. The cloak of practiced disinterest now covered him. Latisha continued, "Five days later, they finally came up with the cover story that it was because Floyd Jackson had attempted to rape a white woman. It took them five days to come up with the oldest story in their old and ugly book. A story that smeared the reputation of a good man. An obviously bullshit story."

"Watch your language, ma'am, or I'll have to ask you to leave."

Latisha stared at Thompson. Though the air conditioner was blasting so hard it was actually a bit chilly in there, a droplet of sweat was trickling down the right side of his forehead.

"Interesting," Latisha said. "The Klan kills an innocent black man. Brutally beats him to death. And what bothers you is a swear word heard in almost every movie in almost every cinema across the nation. Funny, but I'm a lot more offended by murder than cuss words. But that's just me."

"I'm going to have to ask you to leave, young lady." Thompson glowered. "Although you don't seem like much of a lady to me."

Latisha thought of telling him to go fuck himself, thereby removing all doubt as to her lady hood, but instead said, "Is there a Floyd Jackson murder file somewhere in the bowels of this police station? A summary report, at least? Online or perhaps on microfiche? Or would that be off-site somewhere? *Or did Klan killings not even warrant a murder file?*"

Chief Thompson stood, signaling her to leave. A smug grin came over his face.

"What do you think?" he said.

___

THAT WENT WELL.

Latisha glanced at Grandma June's sheet of old community leaders. She picked the top name, Derrick Simpkins, the School Committee chairman back in 1955, put 143 Brooksby Farm Road into her GPS, and headed off. On the way, she glanced into her rear view mirror, checking for a tail, knowing it was paranoia but unable to help herself.

Yes, it wasn't 1955, when Floyd Jackson was getting beaten to death here for no apparent reason other than that he was black. Or fourteen-year-old Emmett Till was getting similarly brutally beaten to death for allegedly flirting with a white woman. It wasn't 1964, when Andrew Goodman, Michael Schwerner, and James Chaney were getting shot and dumped into Mississippi swamps for daring to register black voters. And it wasn't 1968, when Dr. Martin Luther King was being assassinated.

But this remained a scary time to be an African American. The statistics didn't lie. Hatred felt even more rampant than a decade earlier. Sometimes what felt like paranoia was the only thing that could save your black ass.

This time, though, it was just paranoia. Fortunately.

She arrived at 143 Brooksby Farm Road, pulled into an empty driveway, and walked up a gravel walkway through an overgrown lawn to a porch, its cement crumbling. Peering through a picture window into a dark front room in a silent house, she rang the doorbell.

And waited.

And waited.

She rang the bell, then waited some more. Inside, no lights turned on. No footsteps approached.

No luck.

Latisha wouldn't have been surprised if she'd been looking for middle-aged, working people. But Derrick Simpkins was so far past retirement age, he couldn't possibly still be working.

Finally, she gave up and went to the next name on the list. Byron Mayfield.

Same result.

The paranoid thought that Chief Thompson had called both of them and warned them flitted through Latisha's mind, but she rejected it. How would he have known her next steps? How could he have guessed at the contents of Grandma June's list?

Even so, Latisha paid even more attention to her rear view mirror as she headed to the last "live" name on her list, Benjamin Covington.

Once again, no tail materialized. Once again, the lawn was overgrown and the house inside dark. This time, though, a light flicked on, and footsteps approached. Suddenly, Latisha's paranoia manifested itself in the reminder that she was unarmed. She'd flown commercial down here, so her service revolver was back up north. She was pursuing a case with potentially dangerous suspects, but had no weapon.

And no one knew where she was. Except perhaps Chief Thompson and his men. Grandma June might be able to figure it out after the fact, after Latisha's lifeless body was found somewhere. Grandma would assume Latisha had been investigating the three hot leads and put two and two together. But too late.

The approaching footsteps stopped at the front door.

Fingers pulled aside a blind looking out from the front room window.

"Go away," a hoarse voice commanded, then said it again adding the N-word in case she hadn't gotten the message.

"I just want to ask you some questions," Latisha said.

"And I've got a shotgun here that wants to blow a hole in your fucking head."

As Q&A's went, Latisha thought, that was a hell of an answer. She ducked down and raced for her car, halfway expecting the boom of a shotgun blast cutting her in two.

But all she heard was the gravel beneath her feet, the pounding of her heartbeat, and her gasps of breath as she got to Hyundai, wrenched it open, and sped off back in the direction she'd come from.

Time for the library.

***

Latisha figured she had two choices. Call it quits, tell Grandma June she'd done her best, or at least all she felt she could safely or sanely do, and shift back into vacation mode. Or take the inner rage that boiled inside and double down.

Latisha was doubling the fuck down.

She wasn't going to go back to Benjamin Covington's house alone and unarmed. For now, she wasn't even going to go back there at all. Just because he had used the N-word on her and threatened to blow her to kingdom come didn't mean he'd killed Floyd Jackson. He had certainly become Suspect Number One (with a bullet, as her mother had often said way back when), but that didn't mean it was time to close off all other avenues of the investigation. It was time to step back and look at the other possibilities, especially with Covington... unapproachable.

And so, Latisha entered the Charlton Public Library, her heart still partway in her throat, and followed the signs for the reference desk, walking up to the second floor and off to the far left corner where thigh-high, dark wood paneling set off the reference section. She approached a white-haired woman with black-rimmed glasses sitting at a wide gray metal desk facing out. Behind and perpendicular to her desk was a long, battered wooden table with two old-looking, unused computers and a gray microfiche machine. An empty wooden chair sat in front of each. The woman, who wore a plain white blouse, a black skirt, and looked about sixty, frowned at her computer screen. She shook her head.

She looked up, startled. "I'm sorry. May I help you?"

Latisha requested access to the local newspaper archives dating back to August 1955 and the following months.

"Oh, my," the woman said. A black nametag in white print gave her name as Betty Sue Howland. Betty Sue said, "That's a long way back. We don't have that year online. It's on microfiche, some of which has been deteriorating. I'll have to get those spools out of storage. We keep them cold to preserve them as best we can."

Less than a minute later, however, she was back with six cylindrical containers, cold as advertised, in a brown shoebox. "Please be gentle."

Latisha was gentle. For two bleeping hours. Gently, she twisted the black knobs to move from one grainy, blurry black-and-white snapshot of the Charlton Herald, sometimes squinting at the monitor to make out the text.

After a third hour, she gave up.

She certainly hadn't expected a story headlined "KKK Murders Innocent Negro" or anything even remotely like that gift-wrapped for her. Latisha knew her history. Klan attacks might have been covered by the newspapers in the early part of the twentieth century—some lynchings were even announced in advance in the newspapers— but by 1955 it was all done in secret.

So she hadn't expected much. Hints of unrest or other racial problems. Other than, of course, the previous year's *Brown vs. Board of Education* Supreme Court decision. But there had been nothing specific to Charlton or Floyd Jackson. Not a clue before or after his death about what might have precipitated the attack.

All Latisha got was seven more names of marginally prominent Charlton men in 1955 to try. Just seven. Grandma June's research had been even more exceptional than Latisha originally thought. And all seven, an Internet search on her smart phone proved, had passed away.

Latisha wanted to scream. She had nothing.

Nothing, other than the psycho with the shotgun. Benjamin Covington.

Although did she really need anything more? Wasn't "other than the psycho with the shotgun" just like "other than that, Mrs. Lincoln, how'd you like the play?" Latisha had her prime suspect, at least based on his reaction. She couldn't approach him quite yet, but maybe she should just be happy with that for now, and figure out how to actually get to Covington.

Or declare victory and quit. Tell Grandma June that threats of getting blown into two by a shotgun were quite far enough to go in search of clearing a dead man's name.

But declaring such a hollow victory wasn't how Latisha had flown so quickly up the ranks. *Settling* was not her style.

So she turned back to Betty Sue and asked for online access to more current editions of the Charlton Herald, and for some time on the two, still unused, library computers. Betty Sue happily provided the passwords—brightly saying that that was what she was there for—and Latisha got back to work. She searched on the latest local election and scoured the news on the candidates, searching for some connection between 1955 and today.

And found one in a story about the police chief's election. In a total non-coincidence, Police Chief Thompson's grandfather on his mother's side, one Henry Allen Brooks, had not only also been the police chief, but had held that position in 1955.

At first, Latisha had been thrilled at the discovery. But then she realized it did nothing for her effort to understand what had happened to Floyd Jackson and clear his name, other than to make it clear she'd get no police support at all. It only explained why, beyond just general orneriness, Police Chief Thompson had proven so unco-operative.

Which put Latisha back to square one. She had an uncooperative police chief who'd do everything he could to sabotage her investigation, if she actually got anywhere, and a psycho racist who wanted to blow her to bits. But she still didn't know a damned thing about Floyd Jackson.

Dammit! She was getting nowhere. She let out a sigh of exasperation.

"You seem frustrated," Betty Sue said, ten feet off to Latisha's right. Betty Sue had been facing out on the rest of the library's second floor, her back to Latisha, but turned around now to face her. "I'm not trying at all to pry, and I'm really not a snoop, but if you're looking into the town's history, I might be able to help. Or point you to someone who could."

"Thank you!" Latisha said. The sweet little old lady certainly didn't look like she knew anything unsavory about the town, but her offer to point Latisha to someone else sounded promising. It was at least a straw to grasp at.

"Scoot over here," Betty Sue said, pointing to the nearest chair. Latisha moved over.

Betty Sue scanned the library. She turned back to Latisha and leaned close.

"I'm guessing that what you're looking for isn't something... you're going to find in the newspapers."

"Seems not."

"And I may be the only person willing and able to help."

"That would be great."

Betty Sue scanned the room again to make sure the coast was clear.

"If I help you out in any way, you can't let anyone know about it. No one!"

Latisha nodded. Apparently she didn't have a monopoly on paranoia. Betty Sue again checked the room.

"What specifically are you looking for?" Betty Sue asked.

"There was a Klan killing in 1955."

Betty Sue nodded. "Which one?"

Latisha felt her jaw drop and her heart sink. Something deep within her wanted to cry. "There was more than one? In such a little town?"

Betty Sue's eyes fell. "I'm afraid there were. Mind you, this isn't eyewitness testimony I'm giving you. I hadn't even been born in 1955. But... when it comes to this town, I know what I'm talking about."

"How many killings? Two?"

"It might be safest for me if you tell me what you know, and I'll just confirm or deny."

"Three? Four? Good God Almighty, how many?"

"Keep your voice down! There's no one else up here, but if anyone downstairs hears us, I'm finished."

"Sorry."

"I've said far too much already. For all I know, you could be... you could be with them, trying to trap me..."

"I'm a white man in blackface?" Latisha said. "Come on! You know I'm on the right side!"

"Okay, there were five. Five in 1955. It was a bad year. Because of *Brown vs. Board of Education*. People here couldn't come to grips with their children someday sharing classrooms with..." Betty Sue shrugged. "You know, 'the colored.'"

A bitter taste filled Latisha's mouth. Five murdered by

the Klan was a bad year? What was three dead, a medi-ocre one? Par for the fucking course? In a town of five thousand?

She thought about those Klansmen, all those "upstanding citizens" after they took off their white hoods and robes. Leaders of the community. God-fearing individuals who could sing "Amazing Grace" on Sunday after butchering Floyd Jackson just a few days earlier. And murdering four others that same year. Latisha clenched her fists to keep her hands from shaking.

"Which one?" Betty Sue asked, yanking Latisha back into the conversation.

"What were their names?" Latisha hissed. "All of them!"

The librarian shook her head. "I've said way too much. You tell me what you know."

Latisha gave in. "Floyd Jackson."

"I was afraid you'd say that, and yet relieved at the same time. Afraid you'd say that because that's the one I know the least about. That's the one *everyone* knows the least about."

"Why? What do you know?"

"You first."

Latisha told her everything, how she hoped to clear Floyd Jackson's name, if not bring the perpetrators to justice. But she had been running into one brick wall after another. Her only breakthrough was finding out that the current police chief was the grandson of the chief at the time of the murder. And that implicated no one; it only explained Chief Thompson's smug demeanor.

"You're right that the Klan killed Floyd Jackson," Betty

Sue said. "Nobody doubts that. And you're almost certainly right about the rape claim being an invented excuse after the fact. If they had really believed that he tried to rape a white woman, they would have probably cut off his genitals, preferably while he was still alive. And if they hadn't, they certainly would have tortured him... down there.

"And they would have let everyone know along the grapevine about the attempted rape the instant his body was found. Give the reason why it had to be done. Instead, as you correctly point out, it took five days for them to resort to that rationale.

"But mystery still surrounds Floyd Jackson's death. Why did they target him? That's the mystery."

Latisha let it all sink in. After a long while, she asked, "How do you know all this?"

Silence hung heavy in the air. Betty Sue looked all about, then down at her hands.

"Let's just say that my father was an evil man. And my grandfather was even worse. If you had said a name other than Floyd Jackson, your victim's blood could have been on my family's hands. But not Floyd Jackson. About him, I just don't know."

Latisha swallowed hard. This sweet woman came from... that? Did any of that evil still lurk within her?

As if reading her mind, Betty Sue said, "I am not my father's daughter. I am not my grandfather's granddaughter. I am not your enemy. I am so sorry for what they did. I can't begin to repay that debt. But I am different."

A painful silence descended.

"What's your plan now?" Betty Sue finally asked.

"I don't know," Latisha admitted. "I got a list from my grandmother of prominent men back in 1955, hoping one of them was the Klansman that killed Floyd Jackson. I couldn't look for everybody so I used that narrowed-down list." Latisha gestured to the sheets of paper laying on the wooden table between the two computers. "I tried to add some more names using my own research, but they're all dead. Only three of them are still alive and in the area.

"I was hoping to talk to them. Get a death-bed confession, I guess. At least find out why it happened. Do *something* to clear Floyd Jackson's name. But two of them either weren't home this morning or were hiding. The other one, Benjamin Covington, threatened to blow me to pieces with his shotgun. So I don't think I'll be getting anything out of him."

"Let me see your list," Betty Sue said.

Latisha handed it to her.

Betty Sue studied the list. Her eyes went slowly up and down it.

"When you find the guilty person," Betty Sue said, "*if* you find him, you're not going to kill him, are you? Or commit any crime against him?"

"No."

Betty Sue scanned the room.

"You didn't hear this from me, but there's a man not on this list that you want to talk to. You need to talk to him. Soon. But you *absolutely* did not get this from me. Understood?"

Latisha nodded vigorously.

"His name is Lloyd Cooper." Betty Sue drew in a deep

breath. "He's living in a nursing home on Southard Street. Cosgrove Nursing Home. Don't kill him. Don't hurt him. He may not tell you everything you want to know, but if he says he didn't do it... don't believe him."

UNLIKE THE BETTER RETIREMENT FACILITIES WHERE residents actually had money to protect, Cosgrove Nursing Home catered to those whose savings had been drained dry. They couldn't afford anything better. Its security was all but nonexistent primarily because security cost money, and also because its residents had nothing to steal.

After scouting it out from afar, Latisha drove up with three hot pizzas on the Hyundai's passenger seat. She couldn't claim to be Cooper's visiting granddaughter, but acting as a black delivery person would pass muster. She parked the car, signed in at the front desk under the name of Lauren Smith—no ID required—got Cooper's room number on the second floor, and walked up the stairs. The hallway extended for a couple hundred feet, the dark blue carpeting stained and the light yellow paint on the walls peeling. The place really was a dump. It was a warehouse for those just waiting to die.

Latisha knocked on the door and got ready.

"Who is it?" came a voice from the other side of the door. It looked like there was no peep hole.

"Pizza delivery," Latisha called out cheerfully.

"I didn't order no pizza."

"It's from a friend," she said, hoping Cooper had at least one person who'd fit the bill. "Already paid for."

"Already paid for?" the door opened a crack, then slammed shut. A few seconds passed, then it opened a crack again as far as the security chain would allow. "You ain't shitting me? It's paid for? By who?"

"I don't know. I just know I have three large pizzas here that smell awfully good." Latisha held them close to the door. "Cheese, pepperoni, and one with every damned thing on it. You don't want to eat them, I might eat 'em myself. The smell is killing me."

The door opened and Latisha stepped inside. She passed a bathroom on her left, barely suppressing her gag reflex at the smell of urine, feces, and sweat. She strode past a yellow-stained fold-out bed to a small circular kitchen table and set the pizzas on it. Ten feet away, a TV on a wooden stand played Judge Judy.

Behind her, Lloyd Cooper clopped with his walker, trailing a green oxygen canister on small wheels, its tube going up to his nose. He wheezed with every step. He hadn't shaved in days. Yellow stains covered his wifebeater T-shirt.

"Would you like me to get a slice of pizza out for you?" Latisha asked.

"Don't touch it!"

Latisha nodded. "I just have a question or two for you, and I'll be on my way."

Cooper narrowed his eyes. He scratched his whiskered chin. "What questions? You said the pizza was paid for. Get the fuck out of here."

"The pizza were paid for," Latisha said. "But something else wasn't."

"What the fuck are you talking about?"

"Floyd Jackson's murder."

Latisha stared at Cooper. It took a long, long time for the light to dawn.

"That nig—" He stopped, and perhaps assessed his vulnerability. "That Negro? Way back... when the fuck was that?"

"1955."

"That boy's been dead a long time now. What do you want with him? What do you want with me? You some kind of cop? A do-gooder?"

"I just want to find out what happened that night. Then you can get to eating your pizza in peace and quiet. Why'd you good old boys beat him to death? You and I both know that story about him raping a woman was bullshit."

Cooper chuckled, then coughed and begin to choke on his own phlegm. When he finally got control of himself, he said, "Why should I tell you?"

"Get it off your chest. How much longer you got to live? Three months? Four? You got the COPD bad, I can tell. Ain't no way you lasting six months. Get it off your chest."

"I ain't got it on my chest. I don't really care."

"Don't care that you killed a man for nothing?"

"He weren't no man, you ask me," Cooper said, the implication clear.

Latisha wanted to break every bone in his body. Instead, she said, "You're going to tell me why you killed him, or I'm going to take that green tube of oxygen, and I'm going to beat you with it like you beat Floyd Jackson. Beat you into a pulp like you did to Floyd Jackson. Then I'm going to shove it up your ass. Then I might just try to light it on fire. See if it blows." Latisha watched with satisfaction as Cooper squirmed. "Or you can tell me why you killed Floyd Jackson."

"Can I have a slice of pizza?"

"Knock yourself out," Latisha said.

Cooper wolfed down a slice with everything on it, gobbling it like it was his last meal. Grease ran down his chin. He reached for another slice, but Latisha grabbed him by the wrist.

"Talk."

"Okay, okay." Cooper rubbed his wrist as if she'd actually hurt him, the poor baby. "Floyd Jackson knew the rules. All of them did," Cooper said. "Charlton was a sundown town, everyone knew that. Signs everywhere told them, 'Negro, don't let the sun go down on you here.' So when we seen him long after sundown, we had to let him know we mean business.

"He begged and pleaded like they always do. Said he'd shoed a horse and it plum kicked him in the head. Knocked him out cold. Didn't come to until it was well after dark. Said he locked up the barn and hustled on out of there. It had never happened before and it would never happen again.

"Like we was supposed to believe that. They always had a story when we caught them planning to violate our women. A horse kicked him in the head! Can you believe that? That's why I still remember it."

"You beat him to death because he violated the sundown rule?" Latisha said.

"We got a little carried away. Me, mostly, but also the police chief." Cooper laughed. Latisha's blood ran cold. "He had his hood and robes on, but I could tell it was him from his voice, saying as he beat him with a club, 'You think you can stay after dark *in my town*? You think you can stay *in my town*?' Like he owned it, you know?"

Struggling to control herself, Latisha said, "Why the bullshit story about Floyd raping a woman?"

"We got into trouble with the Grand Wizard. Said we shouldn't be killing Negroes just because of the sundown rule. It wasn't like the old times anymore. There was too much attention on us, and it made us look bad. Like that Emmett Till thing in Mississippi just cause the kid was flirting with one of our women. But everyone would understand if rape was the cause. So we made up the story, and no one thought much about it after that."

Latisha clenched and unclenched her hands.

"No one thought much about it?" she asked.

"Not really," Cooper said.

Latisha stood, waves of nausea rolling over her. "Eat your fucking pizza, you piece of shit."

As she walked away, Cooper chuckled.

LATISHA vaulted over the counter at the Charlton police station, brushed past the administrative assistant with the stifling perfume, and barged into the police chief's office.

Chief Thompson shot to his feet. "What the hell do you think you're doing?"

"I hadn't realized that your granddaddy was Chief of Police back in 1955," Latisha said. "When Floyd Jackson was beaten to death by the Klan."

"My family has a long and proud history in law enforcement."

"Does your family also have a long and proud history in the Klan?"

Thompson glared. "I'll have to ask you to leave, Miss Watkins."

"I think you'll want to hear something first."

Thompson froze.

Latisha had preset the recording on her phone at the appropriate mark, past where she had threatened Cooper with his oxygen tank. That unfortunate exchange had forced its erasure and everything that preceded it. But after that, all the good stuff remained. Latisha pressed play.

She watched with satisfaction as Thompson's jaw set, and his face turned red with anger as Cooper explained it all. *We got a little carried away. Me, mostly, but also the police chief. He had his hood and robes on, but I could tell it was him from his voice, saying as he beat him with a club, 'You think you can stay after dark in my town? You think you can stay in my town?' Like he owned it, you know.*

"Give me that!" Thompson demanded, his hand extended.

"Too late," Latisha said. "A copy of it has already been sent to several interested individuals as well as over a dozen newspapers, including the *New York Times*, the

Boston Globe, and the *LA Times*. There's material in there for one helluva feature story, don't you think? Maybe even Pulitzer Prize material. You're going to be famous. You and your grandfather and your long and proud history in law enforcement."

"How did you get that recording? Lloyd Cooper never would have agreed to talk to you."

"As I told you before, I'm off duty. A private citizen. And while a policeman—even one with a long and proud history in law enforcement—is forbidden to secretly record a conversation without a court order, a private citizen is free to do so in Oklahoma. It's a crime in states like"—Latisha cleared her throat—"*Ass*-achusetts. But not here."

Thompson glowered.

"Checkmate," Latisha said.

Teeth gritted and nostrils flaring, Thompson said, "Get out of this room, get out of this police station, and get out of this town."

"With pleasure."

Latisha walked out of the police station and drove happily out of Charlton. It was time to play a recording for Grandma June.

DEVIL IN DISGUISE

INTRODUCTION TO DEVIL IN DISGUISE

When Michael Bracken announced his anthology titled *Groovy Gumshoes: Private Eyes in the Psychedelic Sixties*, my creative subconscious didn't merely begin to salivate. It drooled all over the place. Not only has Michael won countless mystery and suspense awards for his writing and editing, the sixties are square in my wheelhouse.

For most of my life, I've considered it to be the single most fascinating decade, pivotal in so many ways. I've studied it extensively and yes, I did grow up in it (although I was too young to remember all but the last few years). All four of my Young Adult sports novels are set in the late sixties. (Since you asked, that would be *Cracking the Ice, Offside, Offensive Foul,* and *Bottom of the Ninth.*)

So I sat down to my writing computer and was off to the races. The sixties. Private Eyes. A piece of cake. Like taking candy from babies.

My slobbering creative subconscious, however, took

off in an impossible direction. And one thing about that uncontrollable two-year-old is that he goes where he wants to go and isn't about to be told otherwise. He is the boss.

That devilish subconscious did indeed set my private eye smack dab in the psychedelic, bellbottomed groovy sixties—can you dig it, man?—but he also led it down the path of werewolves.

Ruh-roh.

I've worked with Michael Bracken on multiple projects and know for certain that he does *not* want extreme elements of the fantastic in his anthologies. In only the rarest of instances has even the hint of the paranormal snuck in, and in those cases it wasn't crucial to the story. So a werewolf front and center in *Groovy Gumshoes?* Fuhgeddaboudit.

So what the hell was my creative subconscious doing with werewolves? *Werewolves?* Answer: whatever it damned well pleased.

If you read my introduction to "When the Sun Goes Down," you might recall that I contended that a writer needs to follow his vision and tell the tales he wants to tell. And if the first (few) attempts don't match an editor's specifications, you write additional ones that do.

Here is Exhibit A.

"Devil in Disguise" is the *second* story I wrote for *Groovy Gumshoes.* (The first one, "Werewolf Babysitter," was accepted for publication elsewhere but has not yet appeared.) "Devil in Disguise" does not include werewolves or any other element of the fantastic, and Michael bought it for what became *More Groovy Gumshoes.* Sometimes, you see, an editor gets the rare opportunity to release multiple volumes of an anthology when he's flooded with more great stories than can fit into one. Michael and all of his writers were fortunate for that ideal result.

And I consider myself especially fortunate because I let my slobbering creative subconscious run wild and as a reward got to write *two* stories I love.

DEVIL IN DISGUISE

August 7, 1966
Lynn, Massachusetts

I'd never billed a client for hours spent attending church. This was a first. And holy shit, I wasn't charging damned near enough. This was Hell.

The New Testament Church of Holiness was filled to capacity, about two hundred of us trying to keep our elbows out of each other's ribs while sweating our asses off in the dozen rows of white-pine pews. Fans whirring in the three windows on each side tried unsuccessfully to cool the heavy, humid air. I was downwind of the scrawny elderly man seated on my left whose body odor made my eyes water, yet I still caught cross-drafts from the stout middle-aged woman on my right who must have fallen in a vat of cheap perfume. I wondered if they detected remnants of the grass I smoked last night on my clothes or the Jack Daniel's leaking out of my pores.

I stuck out like the proverbial sore thumb. Or perhaps

a middle finger. I'm of average height and weight, but I was the only male with a shaggy, Beatles-style moptop haircut. I was surrounded by military-style crew cuts and short, clean-cut hair, neatly matted in place with "a little dab'll do ya" Brylcreem. My low-slung white pants, light blue shirt, and sandals stood in stark contrast to the dark suits, white shirts, thin ties, and freshly shined shoes all around me. The women, including the perfume-vat on my right, all wore conservative dresses in suitably boring colors appropriate for this Sunday-morning service. There were no pantsuits and certainly no bright-colored miniskirts like the ones I'd enjoyed viewing at the bar last night. No flashy jewelry or makeup. All of that was "worldly."

I'd considered trying to maintain cover by wearing the one rarely used suit I owned, but no way was I getting my hair cut. No freaking way. If a pretty young thing had even a fighting chance of confusing me with Paul McCartney, I wasn't going to sacrifice that. Not for any case, no matter how lucrative. And this one would pay only my minimum fee, if that, because I was helping my friend Gordo.

So I was the one unabashed sinner in the crowd, plain for all to see. I could not have been more conspic-uous if I were naked. I certainly had been getting the disapproving "we'll have to pray for you" looks from all who glanced my way, especially the woman on my right who I'd come to think of as Perfume-Vat Pauline.

Rev. Charles Dinsmore was half an hour into his hell-fire-and-brimstone sermon and gave all the appearance of just warming up. A short, squat, fiery man with black-rimmed glasses, he paced back and forth on the elevated stage, waving his well-worn Bible for emphasis and pushing his glasses back up to the bridge of his nose when they slid down.

He'd begun the sermon attacking that demon woman, Madalyn Murray O'Hair, whose lawsuit had gotten prayer recently removed from the schools and, as a result, we were now going to Hell in a handbasket.

"In the words of Reverend Billy Graham," Dinsmore proclaimed, "if God doesn't soon bring judgment upon America, He'll have to go back and apologize to Sodom and Gomorrah!"

Amens sounded from much of the congregation, including from Perfume-Vat Pauline, who glanced sideways at me with a grim look. My prodigious detective skills told me her glance was not meant to be flirtatious. Just in case, though, I gave her a wink.

"Young men are protesting in the streets and burning their draft cards in defiance of our once-great country," Dinsmore bellowed. "Like their cowardly heavyweight boxing champion, Muhammad Ali, who cast aside his Christian name to take on one of a blasphemous religion, these young men refuse to fight Godless Communism and its spread across the world. Instead, they stomp their feet like spoiled children and chant, 'No, we won't go!' They want nothing more than to stay here where they can live in sin, smoking marijuana, getting drunk, and fornicating with loose women."

Dinsmore had me there. Especially the fornicating.

"Communists like Martin Luther King break the law while they protest the treatment of their race, a race that the Bible tells us God has cursed since the days of Noah and Ham."

I sat up straight on that one, no longer content to crack silent jokes for my own amusement. Taking on Dr. King and the Civil Rights movement was treading on my own sacred ground. Little more than a year ago, I'd driven to Alabama with my friend, Lincoln Bingham, to join the march from Selma to Montgomery to support voting rights. We'd both taken billy clubs to the head, the back, and the ribs for that privilege, and we had the scars to prove it. Some days, I'd swear there were remnants of the tear gas in my lungs.

So Dinsmore had entered my own Don't-Fuck-With-Me zone. And so had the righteous racists in the all-white congregation who were giving him amens and cries of "Preach it Brother!" in response to his attacks on Dr. King.

For me, this was war. I had no idea what the hell Noah had to do with the Civil Rights movement but made a mental note to figure it out.

Dinsmore barreled on.

"'In God We Trust' may be what's printed on our money," he proclaimed, "but the sad reality is that it's the atheists, the depraved hedonists, and the secular humanists who our morally bankrupt government has come to trust!" Dinsmore stopped his pacing and stood behind the pulpit. He leaned on it and glared down with righteous fury from one side of the congregation to the other. His jaw clenched and unclenched. "Nowhere is this more pervasive and insidious than in the depravity of rock and roll, the Devil's music."

Resounding amens rang out.

"Preach it!" Perfume-Vat Pauline called out, raising her arms ostensibly to praise the Lord, but in the process elbowing me in the temple. Seeing stars and shaking my head, I wondered if it had been accidental or if the woman had felt God guiding her elbow to His desired destination.

She tried to apologize, but I waved her away. I wasn't going to be distracted now. This part of Dinsmore's sermon was why I was here. My friend Charlie Gordon—known to his friends as Gordo—owned Gordo's Records here in the city known as "Lynn, Lynn, City of Sin," ten miles north of Boston. He'd hired me a few days ago to get something on Dinsmore, figuring it would be no different than the steady diet of cheating-spouse surveillances I was always bitching about while scouring his record bins. Dinsmore had been killing Gordo's business by directing his parishioners to picket the store ever since John Lennon opened his big mouth and said that the Beatles were more popular than Christ.

The words poured gasoline on Dinsmore's hellfire and brimstone. You could almost smell the sulfur. The words confirmed everything he'd already been preaching about rock and roll. What more proof was needed that this was the Devil's music, and Lennon was Satan's handmaiden?

For Gordo, all Holy Hell broke loose. Only his most loyal customers would cross Dinsmore's righteous picket line, populated with adults and teenagers chanting and shaking placards that bore messages like "Jesus is More Popular to Me!" and "Down with Lennon, Up with Christ!" and then appalling ones that said, "Jesus Lives,

Death to John Lennon!" and "Jesus Died for my Sins! John Lennon should Die For His!"

With the Stones touring to support their new album, *Aftermath*—including an appearance here in Lynn's decrepit Manning Bowl—and the Beatles less than two weeks from hitting Boston to support *Revolver*, Charlie had copies of the two albums stacked high in his store.

Which was where they were staying and would stay if I couldn't get Dinsmore to call off his dogs.

Getting dirt on Dinsmore, however, proved tougher than my typical cheating-spouse cases. As far as I could tell, he wasn't cheating on his wife, either with a horny parishioner or with the prostitutes working Lynn's down-town streets after dark. Dinsmore didn't even sneak a peek at the *Playboy* and *Penthouse* magazines in the third aisle of the Shop Qwik convenience store.

He appeared to be that most annoying of adversaries. He was a world-class asshole, but he was a genuine world-class asshole. One who actually practiced what he preached. So here I was still looking for dirt while paying special attention to his attacks on the music I loved and that kept Gordo in business.

"Just weeks ago, Michael Jagger and his so-called Rolling Stones came to this very city and instigated a riot," Dinsmore said, butchering Mick Jagger's name along with the truth.

Lynn's crumbling Manning Bowl had been the odd site to kick off the Stones' US tour instead of Boston itself or any of the other surrounding cities. Even so, every-thing had gone fine from host Arnie "Woo Woo" Ginsburg to the opening acts to the Stones themselves. Ten thousand people having a great time.

Until the thunderstorms hit.

The Stones had just finished their tenth song, "(I Can't Get No) Satisfaction," when the heavy rain turned into a deluge and the thunder struck. Mick and the boys ran for cover. Fans rushed the stage and broke through the police barriers. Next thing you knew, the police were firing tear gas, the Stones were leaving in their limos, and wooden chairs were flying all about the infield.

The Stones said they'd never return, the newspapers reported the "riot," and "Lynn, Lynn, City of Sin" had once again lived up to its name. And given more ammo to Dinsmore, a self-appointed missionary intent on converting our City of Sin.

"John Lennon thinks you love his Beatles more than you love your Lord and Savior who died on the cross to save you from your sins!" Dinsmore bellowed. "But we know better! The Beatles have come, and they will go, but our Lord God is eternal! John Lennon will burn in Hell for his sins! Do not follow him to eternal damnation!"

AFTER THE SERVICE, the bonfire in the large gravel parking lot behind the church leaped high into the sky, as if symbolizing John Lennon roasting like a marshmallow in Hell. The acrid smell of burning vinyl filled my nostrils. Ashes from the paperboard album covers wafted lazily through the heavy air toward the cars parked on the perimeter.

The congregation circled the bonfire, six or seven deep, fifteen feet back from the bright orange flames. I stood with the adults and little children on the outer edges looking in, them approvingly at the teenagers holding their albums and waiting their turn, me in silent horror. I wondered if any of the teenagers felt fenced in by their elders, unable to escape, forced to follow the commands of Dinsmore, who stood on a folding metal chair on the far side of the circle with the shittiest of shit-eating grins.

I wanted to slap him.

One after another teenager, and more than a few adults, took their turn and stepped forward to add their sacrifice to the bright orange flame. Always one album at a time, never more than one, not even a brown-haired girl who couldn't have been more than fourteen yet had a stack of close to thirty albums. I cried for her as she flung each album in and watched it warp and burn.

I wanted to call out, "*What are you doing?*" and probably should have. Was I worrying that I'd blow my cover, a cover that had been blown as soon as I showed up here without a haircut? Even so, I couldn't flaunt my disapproval of and actual disgust for what was happening. I had to remain within striking distance.

So I just watched. And felt a silent scream build up inside me as if I were watching a Hitchcock film. This was worse than *The Birds* or even Norman Bates in *Psycho*.

The event turned from quiet and reverential to raucous. A bit like a rock concert.

A few boys took to stomping their albums into pieces before flinging them into the fire. The crowd cheered lustily. So a few girls followed suit. Then they all began to hold their albums up first for all to see, showcasing their sacrifice before the stomping.

The crowd chanted, "Let it burn! Let it burn!"

A tall, thin, acne-pocked boy of about sixteen held aloft a copy of *Beatles for Sale*. I almost cried out in pain. The title had only been released in the UK and was a priceless collectors' item in the US. But it went crunch underneath the kid's shoe, and the crowd joyfully chanted, "Let it burn! Let it burn!"

I felt sick to my stomach. This was depravity. Not careless words by John Lennon. This!

I couldn't help thinking of Ray Bradbury's novel about book-burning, *Fahrenheit 451*. Supposedly, François Truffaut would be coming out with the movie version later this year, but I doubted if anyone here but me would go to see it. Hollywood, after all, like rock and roll, was the Devil's playground. Off limits, a temptation that would steal your soul. Besides, would anyone here even recognize themselves as the books burned?

Finally, the sickening event began to wind down. Only the reluctant stragglers were left. A teenaged boy or girl would look longingly at an album that had no doubt been a favorite. They loved the music. They loved the Beatles, or the Stones, or Bob Dylan or whoever the artist was. But then the crowd urged them on even louder.

"*Let it burn! Let it burn! Let it burn!*"

Off to the right, a tear streaked down a plump teenage girl's cheek. She was probably about sixteen or so with short, drab hair. She stared longingly at the cover of *Meet the Beatles*. I wondered if her crush was on Paul or John.

"Don't be like Lot's wife," Rev. Dinsmore commanded.

The girl's head shot up. She stared at Dinsmore and visibly gulped.

"Lot's wife was turned to a pillar of salt when she looked back on the flames devouring Sodom and Gomorrah."

The girl's eyes widened. Her hands trembled.

"Let it burn! Let it burn! Let it burn!"

The girl flung the album into the fire as if it had been diseased. Her eyes blinked back the tears.

GORDO WAS FUCKED.

He was going against the most ardent of the true believers. Unless Dinsmore went down in flames, his parishioners were going to picket Gordo's Records into bankruptcy.

Perhaps some, or even many, of those who had burned their albums would be replacing them, especially after they left home for college, where they'd no longer be under the thumb of their parents. And for the boys, unless they had a medical deferment like me, they'd be going to college or else they'd be packing off to Vietnam.

College would be a whole new world. Many of them would be delivering a hidden fuck-you to Dinsmore and their parents as they rolled a joint and sang along with Bob Dylan, "Everyone must get stoned!"

But Gordo's Records would be long gone by then. Unless I could get something on Dinsmore.

And I still had nothing. Dinsmore was an asshole, but

he did all his assholery in public. He had no secrets that I could detect to expose or leverage.

I felt powerless.

One thing did nag at me, however: Dinsmore's comment about Noah and Ham. I knew Noah. Everyone does. But who the hell was Ham? Or Nam, or something like that. And whatever could Ham, Nam, or for that matter, Damn, have to do with Martin Luther King and the Civil Rights movement?

I'd been born with the most Irish Catholic name possible—Brendan Shamus O'Donnell—and I'd gone to St. Pius and gotten my knuckles rapped by the nuns like everyone else. But all I could remember about Noah was the Flood and the animals in the ark. That was it.

I was lost. No one would ever confuse me with a Biblical scholar, and none of my cases had ever involved theology. I didn't have the first idea of where to look.

So the next morning, I hit the public library. I struck out with the card catalog. Not a single relevant index card. But there was still the librarian, a sweet elderly woman named Miss Emily McLeod who I'd known from Mass at St. Pius back when I was, in her words, "knee-high to a grasshopper." I'd gotten to know her quite well since. Frail with white hair, bony liver-spotted hands, and granny glasses, she was still sharp as a tack, loaded with information that couldn't be found in the stacks, and a bit of a pistol in her own way. She'd provided useful information for me in several cases, and each time that I'd come back to thank her, she'd taken me up on payment via a Guinness or two or three at Casey's.

Usually three.

"Brendan O'Donnell, what can I do for you this fine day?" she asked. "And would it by chance involve something *legal* this time?"

I asked her about Noah and Ham, Nam, Damn, or even "Rama Lama Ding Dong," the last one tossed in for levity because Miss McLeod was a doo-wop fan.

"By the Edsels," she said without even the blink of an eye. "Their biggest hit."

"Sharp as ever," I said. "Had to look that one up myself."

"Clearly, you're better at music than theology. Not surprising since you haven't been to Mass is, oh, about a decade." She lifted her eyebrows in silent accusation.

I was about to defend myself by saying that I'd been to church just yesterday but wasn't sure if going to a hellfire-and-brimstone Protestant church would be considered a greater evil for an Irish Catholic boy than staying home and getting drunk by noon. So I spread my hands in a gesture of pleading the fifth.

"I do remember Noah," I said. "It's the other guy I'm not sure about. And what the he—um... what the heck does he have to do with Martin Luther King?"

"You don't remember that from catechism?" Miss McLeod asked with a sly grin.

All I remembered from catechism was that I should feel guilty about everything, but I didn't say that. I just shrugged sheepishly.

"That's because they don't cover it in catechism," she said with a grin and a wink. "One of those dirty secrets left undiscovered."

"I'm all about dirty secrets," I said. "Especially the undiscovered ones."

"So I've heard," she replied. "I'm getting thirsty for a Guinness already."

"You're on!"

"Ham was one of Noah's sons, and it says in Genesis that Noah got drunk one day and Ham saw Noah's nakedness. Whatever that's supposed to mean." Miss McLeod gave me the eye but continued. "As a result, Noah cursed Ham and his descendants, some of whom supposedly populated Egypt and Africa. Hence, God cursed all Negroes."

"*What?*"

Miss McLeod pursed her lips and raised her eyebrows. "The Curse of Ham has been used to excuse slavery. God's will for a cursed race."

I stood there in stunned silence. I didn't even know what the hell "seeing Noah's nakedness" meant, much less make sense of all the rest.

"Not exactly Christianity's finest moment," Miss McLeod said. "I could, of course, be distorting it just a bit based on my recollections. It's not something Father O'Sullivan brings up often in his homilies.

"You could get a less biased view—or perhaps it would be an equally or even more biased view in *favor* of the Curse—by going to the library at Gordon College," she said, referring to an evangelical school ten miles away. "It's the Winn Library, I believe. It may only be open to students, but I can place a call and perhaps get you in."

My confusion was far more basic than getting both

sides of the issue. I wasn't sure I even wanted both sides of the issue.

"Why was it Ham's fault that Noah got drunk and got naked?" I asked.

Miss McLeod glanced about to make sure no one could overhear.

"Some say that 'seeing Noah's nakedness' is a euphemism." She widened her eyes and craned her head forward, leading me on. "For... you know what."

My eyes bugged out. I could not have been more floored if Muhammad Ali had nailed me with a round-house hook.

"And Noah is the *righteous* guy God supposedly saved in the Flood? Because everyone else was wicked?" I asked, incredulous. "That's supposed to make sense? And his curse is a justification for slavery?"

"Like I said, a dirty secret."

THE NEXT AFTERNOON, having called and scheduled an appointment, I met with Rev. Dinsmore in his office in the back of the church. Dressed in a dark suit and tie as if it were still Sunday, he sat behind a huge desk cluttered with papers. The wall behind him was a floor-to-ceiling bookcase made of white pine and filled with reference books and theological texts. Sunlight and a light breeze streamed in the large, open window on my left. The wall on my right held framed photographs of Dinsmore with apparently important people that I didn't recognize along with a cover each from *Christianity Today* and *Guideposts* magazines.

Dinsmore pointed me to a chair, and I sat down, a Bible in my lap.

"What can I help you with, my son?" he asked. Before I could respond, he said, "I could recommend a good barber." He flashed his shit-eating grin.

I ignored the quip about my hair and said that I was confused about a few things in the scriptures and needed his help to understand. I softened him up with some easy questions until he visibly relaxed, then slipped in a tough one I remembered from my youth.

It got the predictable, "God works in mysterious ways."

More softies, then a tough one from Miss McLeod got another predictable response: "Our finite minds cannot pretend to know the infinite."

One last softie. Then the question I'd come here for.

"You mentioned the Curse of Ham in your sermon on Sunday," I said. "I've read that part of Genesis so many times, but I still don't understand it. Could you explain that to me?"

I was afraid I'd get the kind of non-answer I'd gotten to previous tough questions, but Dinsmore felt no need for evasive action here. He jumped right in.

"Sure," he said. "The Old Testament says quite clearly and in several places that the sins of the father are carried on to the third and fourth generations. Now that may sound harsh, but Deuteronomy 24:16 also says that fathers shall not be put to death because of their children, nor shall children be put to death for their fathers.

So there are limits. But without question, our children do inherit our sins.

"In the case of Ham, he disrespected his father Noah, and as a result, God has punished Ham's descendants. They are not put to death, but they bear that curse. The people of Africa and Egypt are descendants of Ham, and they bear God's curse."

He leaned forward.

"Anyone can see that the Negro man is inferior to the white. I'm sure that even Martin Luther King would agree that his own followers, however loyal and sincere as they may be, fail to measure up intellectually and morally to those in this congregation. It's God's will that we lead those who have not been blessed with the same talents as have we.

"Sometimes, it's even a burden. As it says in the Gospel of Luke, 'To whom much is given, much will be required.'"

I blinked. So there it was. I hardly needed anything more.

Dinsmore was no benign, lonely Father McKenzie from the Beatles' "Eleanor Rigby." Dinsmore was evil even if he didn't think so. And I had the words to bury him.

Perhaps though, I thought, he could add an exclamation point to his statement of bald bigotry.

"That's so much clearer than what you said on Sunday," I said. "Thank you."

Dinsmore smiled and shrugged.

"In private, I can be a little more blunt and speak the plain truth," he said. "At times from the pulpit, I must be a bit more tactful and circumspect. I'm sure you understand."

THE NEXT SUNDAY, I was back to the concrete steps of the New Testament Church of Holiness, but I was not alone.

Protests cut both ways.

I was joined by Lincoln Bingham, my fellow veteran of billy clubs on the Selma march, and almost a hundred members of the African Full Gospel Church.

I also had an edited tape with the highlights of my conversation with Dinsmore recorded by the cassette player I'd hidden inside my hollowed-out Bible the day I'd met with him.

Also, a bullhorn.

I pressed play and held the recorder up to the bullhorn's microphone. The tape was distorted and scratchy, but Dinsmore's words were clear, repeated in a loop over and over again and amplified through my bullhorn.

"The people of Africa and Egypt are descendants of Ham and they bear God's curse. Anyone can see that the Negro man is inferior to the white. I'm sure that even Martin Luther King would agree that his own followers, however loyal and sincere as they may be, fail to measure up intellectually and morally to those in this congregation. It's God's will that we lead those who have not been blessed with the same talents as have we."

Over and over.

Now, on the steps of his church with his congregation slowly spilling outside as they heard his recorded words, Dinsmore took two strides toward me, and our chests thumped. Our faces were inches apart. I could smell onions on his breath.

"What do you want?" he asked, his eyes narrowed, burning fiery.

Originally, I had hoped to trade the ceasing of one protest for another. But Dinsmore's grotesque words and beliefs demanded more now.

"Nothing short of your resignation."

THAT FIRST SUNDAY, the two congregations almost came to blows. Police arrived and forced us to move back to the sidewalks, twenty feet from the church steps. Dinsmore commanded them to arrest us, and for a moment, they appeared ready to do so. Lincoln and I, however, countered that the sidewalks in front of the church were every bit as much public property as those in front of Gordo's Records. We had the right of lawful assembly.

Dinsmore did not resign. The protests that next week in front of Gordo's continued.

The following Sunday, our protest returned in full force, this time joined by Gordo himself, short and thin with thick curly black hair, and even more importantly, photographers and reporters from the city's newspaper, the *Daily Evening Item*, along with a few other suburban papers. And once again, a police presence to keep the peace.

The third Sunday, the *Boston Globe* arrived. Dinsmore called off the pickets of Gordo's Records and claimed to be misunderstood. But the true Devil had been exposed.

The fourth Sunday, Dinsmore submitted his resignation. He would leave immediately for a more "hospitable" location for his ministry. I took that to mean somewhere near Selma, Alabama. Ideologically, if not geographically.

Sadly, though, there were all too many locations like that, places that would welcome him with open arms. Too many people here who had embraced his ideas even to the point of accepting the Curse of Ham.

We'd saved Gordo's business, but that seemed secondary now. We'd won this battle, but the fight that really mattered was just beginning.

I needed a Guinness. Or three.

GACACA

INTRODUCTION TO GACACA

This story arose out of my trip of a lifetime with family members to Africa. Specifically to Rwanda and Tanzania. As magnificent, thrilling, and entertaining as Tanzania's Serengeti proved to be—the TV documentaries pale in comparison to being there—Rwanda's Genocide Memorial Center in Kigali was even more sobering and heartbreaking. The former unforgettable in all the most delightful ways; the latter unforgettable in all the most gut-wrenching ways.

(In fairness, Rwanda also included a wonderful trek into its mountains where we spent time with silverback gorillas, made famous by Dian Fossey. I even received what I call a "hip check" from the three-hundred-fifty pound alpha silverback who wanted to make sure I knew who was boss. As if there was any doubt.... But for me, our time in Rwanda will always be first and foremost about those hours in the Genocide Memorial that flooded my emotions and took my breath away. Afterward, outside, I could barely speak. Could only shake my head and say softly, "Oh my God. Oh my God. Oh my God.")

Inevitably, I wound up writing about both countries and those experiences. Our safari through Tanzania's Serengeti inspired arguably my most famous short story, "Death in the Serengeti," which won a Derringer Award for Best Long Story and was also selected for the prestigious *Best American Mystery Stories 2018*. Rwanda gave birth to the story you're about to read, which first appeared in *Mystery, Crime, and Mayhem: Passionate Crimes*. And together, the two countries and all those experiences combined for my hockey romance *No Defense*. (A hockey romance in Africa? *Hockey? In Africa? How could that be?* Well, Hendrickson says with a mischievous chuckle, you'll just have to read it to find out. Heh, heh, heh.)

GACACA

I was pretty once.

Back then, when Kwizera Bizimungu turned his head and saw me in the row behind him in church, eighteen years old and dressed in my white-and-blue-flowered sundress, my eyes chocolate-brown and my teeth bright white as I smiled back at him, he thought I was the most beautiful girl in all of Rwanda.

That is what he told me later. I remember it still. The most beautiful girl in all Rwanda.

He kept singing the hymn and clapping his hands along with the other four hundred in the congregation, but a wide smile spread across his handsome face. He was seated across the aisle on the wooden bench in front of mine, a head taller than most of the other young men, and so very distinguished in his dark blue suit, white shirt, and matching tie. His hair was close cropped, as mine has always been, and I might have thought that he was the most handsome man in all Rwanda.

"Mutesi Munyakazi, such a beautiful name," he said,

after introducing himself following the service and then hearing my reply. I had managed to separate myself from my family, and we stood alone together on the broad, brick courtyard outside the church, the large white statue of Jesus looking down upon us, arms held out in benediction twenty meters overhead.

"Mutesi Munyakazi," Kwizera said again, and shook his head as if it were as great a wonder as the sun rising in the morning and setting in the evening, leaving behind the stars to twinkle in the black African sky. "The most beautiful girl in all Rwanda."

Oh, he was a charmer. I felt a shiver race up and down my spine, even though the noonday sun beat down hot, and the air was thick.

"So, what about me?" he asked when I remained silent, my tongue tied. And then he laughed the most infectious laugh I had ever heard. Joyful. Filled with the love of life.

And after a dumbfounded silence that almost went too long, I said, "You are *not* the most beautiful girl in all Rwanda."

We laughed and laughed.

My father did not like him at first, because Kwizera was Tutsi and we were Hutu. There were almost six Hutu to every Tutsi, but though they were the majority, many Hutu disliked the Tutsi because in the past they had too many of the best jobs in government. Or something like that. They said the Tutsi were not true Rwandans; they came from Ethiopia. I even heard my father say that once when I was a little girl, so it must be true, but I didn't care.

Some people said that you could tell by looking at

someone which group they were from, that Tutsi were lighter-skinned and had more narrow noses and chins, which is why the colonialists liked them better, but Kwizera was as dark-skinned as I was, and my nose and chin were no broader than his. I guess that's why the government needed identity cards to tell Hutu and Tutsi apart.

But though my father didn't approve at first of me falling in love with a Tutsi, Kwizera won him over, bringing gifts of fruits and chocolates to our house. He would say that the chocolate was because of my choco-late-brown eyes, and then he would laugh. Eventually my father's scowl was replaced with a grudging grin, and then a broad smile. Kwizera had a good job at the National Bank in Kigali, and though he was only twenty-three and had just moved here to take that job, he already owned property in Shyorongi, where he planned to build a house as soon as he had the money.

I did not care about the money, although my father did. I just loved Kwizera with all of my heart.

We were married in the same church where we'd first met, on a bright, shining, glorious day. April 4, 1993. Father Thomas, the senior priest, did not perform the ceremony, leaving it for a junior priest. I thought, even then, that Father Thomas did not approve of a Hutu marrying a Tutsi, but I did not care. We were in love. It mattered little to us which priest gave us God's blessing.

Although we were not favored with children that first year, we were so very happy together. We joined our bodies in love and pleasure many, many times each week. I would hold Kwizera in my arms and rest my head on his bare chest, or if there was light, look into his beautiful, large brown eyes. He would tell me he loved me, and I would match those words with my own.

We moved into our new house in Shyorongi. It was at the end of a long dirt road with a thick forest behind it. We owned no automobile or bicycle, so we walked over an hour into Kigali to get to our jobs, Kwizera at the bank, and me at the second-hand clothes store I was opening, but we didn't mind. We walked together, the smell of woodsmoke and charcoal in the air, and sometimes hand in hand, talking about the future, and sometimes not.

It was all good.

I knew I would give Kwizera many babies, and we would grow old and fat and prosperous together. Our babies would grow up, and then have babies themselves. And on all their birth dates we would enjoy a great feast of celebration and dancing, and we would sing the songs of our Rwandan ancestors, the heritage of our people.

TWO NIGHTS after our first wedding anniversary, the President's plane was shot down.

Kwizera and I knew nothing of this until a tall, young, angry-looking member of the *Interahamwe*, the militia, armed in camouflage fatigues, showed up at the front door of our new house, eyes narrowed, asking for our identity cards. We produced them.

He took a long, cold look at Kwizera.

My sweet Kwizera.

The militia member told us not to leave the house,

spun, and left. With our hearts pounding, we raced to the radio, turned it on, and learned what we could. The President and all aboard the airplane were dead. By the sounds of everything spoke and unspoken, a Hutu extremist who hated the Tutsi was seizing power.

"Did you see the look on his face?" Kwizera asked. "I am a dead man if I stay here."

"There have been problems before," I said, feeling no conviction in my words, just wishing them to be true.

"Did you see his look?" Kwizera repeated.

I had seen it.

"I can't stay here," Kwizera said. "You will be okay. You are Hutu. But I must go."

"Do not leave without me," I said.

"You will be safer here."

I thought of a recent teaching at the church, and the words of the Biblical Ruth came to me.

"Wither thou goest, I will go."

UNDER THE COVER OF DARKNESS, we slipped out the back door and crept into the thick forest behind our house. We escaped undetected, and headed to the church, a sanctuary in the past during conflicts, sometimes violent, between Hutu and Tutsi.

The church was always the safest of safe havens.

We approached its dark red brick façade, crouched in the darkness, looking both ways as we crossed the brick courtyard. I felt great comfort as I looked up to the outstretched arms of Jesus, the pale white statue overhead visible even in the darkness, welcoming us into the safety of His arms.

I held my breath as we raced up the ten brick steps leading to the black wooden front door. If it was locked, we would have to sneak around back or find some other place to hide until daybreak, at which point the doors would surely open to us.

We didn't have to wait. The doors swung wide open and we stepped inside.

We blinked at the lights, then quickly closed the door behind us.

Inside fifty others milled about the thirty rows of pews—short, backless benches made of reddish-brown wood—separated by a middle aisle. At first, they looked at us in wide-eyed alarm, but then nodded in recognition and sighed with relief. The front of the church, the platform and altar, were empty.

"We made it!" I said, turning and hugging my sweet Kwizera for the last time.

SEVERAL HOURS AFTER DAYBREAK, Father Thomas addressed us from the platform. He had emerged from a side door, grim-faced, not wearing the vestments we all saw him in on Sundays, but instead wearing all-black garb with a clerical collar. He was short and squat, with a chubby face and glasses, a large chest, and an even larger protruding belly. The crowd looking back at him had grown to over a hundred, an even split between men and women, but no children.

Father Thomas scanned the crowd.

"Are there any Hutu here?" he asked, and fear shot up and down my spine. A foul, sour taste formed in my mouth. Why was Father Thomas asking that? Was he going to send me home, separating me from Kwizera? Why? There was plenty of room.

Slowly, fearfully, I raised my hand, looking about to see if I were the only one. I concluded that I was when I turned around to face Father Thomas.

A look of hatred filled his face. "Ah yes, Mutesi." He shook his head, as if in disgust. After surveying the rest of the crowd, he nodded.

"I need the women to come up here to the altar," he said. "Mutesi, you, too. Women only. Men, back up."

I looked to Kwizera in bewilderment and fear. What was the meaning of this?

Kwizera's eyes were filled with alarm, but he nodded. "Go ahead," he said softly. "Listen to the Father."

Kwizera turned and stepped over a succession of the long red-brown wooden benches until he and all the other men filled the back four rows, from the middle aisle out to the dark red brick walls. Behind them was only the wall and the large, black door from which they all had entered.

Father Thomas strode toward the men. When he reached them, they parted, crowding in against each other, and he reached the door.

He opened it.

The *Interahamwe*, the militia, piled in, one after another, until they outnumbered the men two to one. They surrounded the half of the men to the left of the door and another group surrounded the half to the right.

Father Thomas closed the door.

The machetes flashed.

They hacked at necks.

They hacked at arms held up to shield heads and necks.

They hacked at anything and everything.

Blood spurted into the air. Men and women alike screamed. The men in pain, the women in panicked terror.

I ran for my Kwizera.

Our eyes met as a blade slashed across his throat.

"Run!" he cried, but then his words bubbled. His eyes rolled back. He collapsed to the floor.

"No!" I screamed.

An *Interahamwe* stepped in my path, and drove the butt of his machete into my forehead.

My legs collapsed beneath me, and my world went all black.

I AWOKE with a man on top of me.

Raping me.

At first, I couldn't figure it out. I didn't know where I was. I didn't know what had happened. My eyes failed to focus. A painful beam of white light shot through my mind.

I felt a stabbing pain between my eyes.

I felt a stabbing pain between my legs.

And then I realized.

I screamed.

Naked, I strained against the arms that held me down. Even as my eyes failed to see anything but pulses of painful bright white light, I screamed, "Stop it! Help me! Someone help me!"

Somewhere in the distance, I heard laughing, and then applause. "The *inyenze* is awake!" The cockroach is awake. "She's awake!"

I fought to get my arms free but I couldn't. "Help me!"

And then...

And then...

When he finished, the vile pig crawled off me. I scrambled to all fours.

I staggered to my feet, still unable to see clearly. My head spun. Pain spasmed from my private parts. My legs shook and I thought I would collapse.

"She's a live one!" I heard someone say from behind me.

For the briefest instant, I thought of Kwizera. He would rescue me. My sweet Kwizera would come save me.

But then I remembered the machete blade across his throat. And the spurting blood. The eyes rolled back. Him falling to the floor.

Dead. My sweet Kwizera would not be coming to my rescue.

I staggered toward what I thought might be the front door, but then strong hands flung me back down.

And I knew I was in Hell.

AT SOME POINT, I realized I was not alone in my violation. All around me, women screamed and thrashed and fought against those assaulting them.

And finally they just cried. Wracking sobs of grief.

As did I.

Until Father Thomas appeared over me.

I blinked, thinking I had surely been sent to Heaven if Father Thomas was looking down upon me, sliding his glasses up to the bridge of his broad nose. But then...

How could there be rape in Heaven?

And the smelly monster on top of me now was most certainly raping me. Grunting and screaming, *"Inyenze!"* over and over. Cockroach! Cockroach! Cockroach!

I realized that I was back here in Hell and...

Father Thomas was watching it all.

"Father!" I screamed. "Help me! Help me!"

Even as the monster on top of me continued, Father Thomas shook his head in disdain.

"You were born Hutu, but defiled yourself by marrying a Tutsi," he said calmly as if giving a closing benediction. "The God of the Hutus hears not your cries. The God of the Tutsis is as dead as your husband."

I AWOKE CHAINED TO A BED, a straw roof close over my head. I pulled at each of the four chains, but they were strong and didn't budge. Beneath me, a mattress stank of urine and days-old raw fish and even worse, of sex. It poked its springs into my back. Fragrant eucalyptus leaves covered my naked body.

I was in a tiny, windowless shack with little space for anything but the metal bed frame to which I was chained. The air was hot and heavy. It hung like a wet cloud over me, filled with the stench of rotting fish. There was no cooling breeze to clear it away.

"You are mine," the man said when he saw that I was awake. He was a big, middle-aged man with glasses and a thick, hairy chest. "I bought you from the *Interahamwe*, but if you are not nice to me, I will share you with all of them." He nodded. "All of them. One after another."

"No, please, not that," I said. "I will be nice to you. I swear it. I will be nice."

He came to me almost every day, always smelling of rotting fish. His clothes reeked of it. So did his skin. It smelled so bad I thought his skin must be made of scales. The stench was even in his close-cropped hair.

The hut stank of fish even after he left. But it also stank of his semen.

Each time, he bathed me and fed me, though never with less than two chains locked. Then he would secure the other locks and climb atop me.

He made me say that I loved him.

He made me pretend that I liked it.

I wanted to kill him. I wanted to die.

I almost told him I couldn't do it. That I could never, ever pretend that I liked it. Never again.

But then I thought of that night again at the church. A night forever burned in my nightmares. And I thought of his threat. *All of them.*

And so I told him I loved him. I pretended that he was the world's greatest lover.

I hated myself even more than I hated him.

ONE DAY, I heard his last name.

He brought a friend to share me with and outside the hut, as they approached, the friend casually mentioned the name.

Bunani.

I heard a slap and my captor said, "Are you insane?"

I acted as though I'd heard nothing, but locked the name away.

Bunani.

ONE NIGHT, he unchained me from the bed. He kept my hands and feet locked together, however, then blindfolded me and led me outside the shack for the very first time. I felt the cool breeze against my naked skin. The crickets chirped in what must have been a very large field.

He—*Bunani*—threw a large, rough robe over me, and led me away from the shack.

"I should kill you now, but I won't," he said. "It is because I love you."

By rote, I repeated the words I'd spoken so often, words that poured searing acid over my soul. "I love you, too."

"You do not love me," he said. "Not the way that I love you."

"I do love you. I do. I do." I hated the pleading in my voice.

I heard the flick of a match, then smelled fire.

He's going to burn me alive, I thought and began to shiver. *After all this, he's going to burn me alive.*

But I feared only the pain, and that only a little. What more could be done to me?

I welcomed death. I longed for its embrace.

Instead, he—*Bunani*—led me to an automobile, dumped me in the trunk, and drove a very long time over very bumpy grounds. All the time, I smelled the fish.

When we stopped, he left my blindfold on but unlocked my cuffs, lifted me out of his trunk, and threw me onto the rocky ground.

As I lay there, he climbed back into his automobile and raced away.

The rebels, the Rwandan Patriotic Front, found me two days later, and brought me to the hospital.

———

AFTER THE RPF TOOK CONTROL, I reported the crimes committed against me, but they were mere grains of sand in a mountain as tall as Kilimanjaro. In the one hundred days of our country's descent into madness, almost one million were killed. Half a million women were raped.

Half a million women like me.

Many of the rapes had been with the intent to kill. Genocide by rape. Seventy percent of the victims developed HIV. I suppose I am fortunate that I am not one of them, but I do not feel fortunate. Everywhere I go, my nightmares follow, filled with the *Interahamwe* taking their turns with me...with Father Thomas watching in approval...and with the man I knew as Bunani.

And so, when I heard of the United Nations' call for an International Tribunal to investigate all facets of the Genocide, I rejoiced. It would not bring back my sweet Kwizera or repair what had been done to me and to so many others, but the world would hear of what was done. It would demand justice.

I wrote letters, and even imagined that I might be called to testify. I would be transported to the tribunal—perhaps even by airplane!—all the way down to Arusha in Tanzania, and I would tell of Father Thomas and the *Interahamwe* and the rich Mr. Bunani – Karegeya Bunani, owner of fish markets all throughout the Bugasera District, as it turned out, a powerful man who no one seemed interested in throwing in jail.

But the Tribunal turned a deaf ear to women like me. We were not of sufficient importance. There were too many of us. While it did declare that rape was no longer the spoils of war, and while it did charge Father Thomas, he escaped to France, like several other priests, and now may face no punishment at all.

None at all for opening the doors of the church for the *Interahamwe*. None at all for standing aside while the militia members slaughtered men like my beloved Kwizera. None at all for watching with approval as they took turns violating women like me.

Women like me are not even worth an apology from the Pope. According to what I have read in the newspaper, if you are an American or European boy who has been molested by a priest, you were consoled by Pope Benedict with these words:

"You have suffered grievously, and I am truly sorry. I know that nothing can undo the wrong you have endured. Your trust has been betrayed, and your dignity has been violated."

But African women who have seen their families slaughtered and their bodies violated inside the churches, sometimes with the explicit permission or cooperation of the priests, deserve nothing?

And while the atrocities done to me, Category I crimes, warrant justice in the traditional Rwandan courts if not the International Tribunal, there is no room for them.

What does a country do when all but twenty of its judges have been killed or have fled its borders? What does it do when so many of its people are guilty that it can't begin to fit them in the jails? What does it do when it would take over a hundred years to try all of the accused?

And so our country, bloodstained and violated, has returned to its old tradition of *gacaca* courts, which is to say "justice in the grass." Communities all across Rwanda gather in groups of about two hundred men and women, sitting on grassy hills and beneath tattered canopies to mete out justice.

The International Tribunal has failed me. The conventional Rwandan courts have failed me. And the Church has sorely failed me.

And so I go to the *gacaca* courts for justice.

I TRAVEL to the Bugasera District where the monster, Karegeya Bunani, lives so I can seek my justice in the *gacaca* court of his community. I know none of the two hundred or so men and women who will determine his fate, and therefore my own. I know none of the nine judges who sit on a long, wooden bench behind a table upon which they put their notes, yellow-and-blue stoles draped over their shoulders, the vestments of their office emblazoned with the word *INYANGAMUGAYO*.

Half of the people gathered here, mostly younger men clad in Western clothes—T-shirts with symbols of Adidas, Nike, and Abercrombie on them—sit on a grassy hillside. Others sit on wooden chairs and benches beneath a faded gray tent-like canopy, its loose threads lightly flapping in the light breeze beneath the hot sun. Some men wear dark suits and ties. Most of the women, including myself, have chosen the traditional African attire of brightly colored long robes and headdresses, though mine are a drab, dark brown.

For these people, it is their duty to gather here. But I need no duty to bring me here today.

The President of the panel stands. He is a handsome young man, perhaps twenty-five, much like my Kwizera Bizimungu except for his shaved head and the jagged scar on his left temple. He wears a plain white shirt and khaki trousers. But he looks impressive and sounds it, too.

"As is our custom before we start these proceedings, we must remember our loved ones who perished in the

Genocide," he says, looking all about at the people gathered here. "We must insure that it never happens again. And so I demand that those wearing hats remove them, and we bow our heads and observe one minute of silence."

The minute passes. He asks for the names of all victims and witnesses, then for us to identify ourselves. I am surprised that in addition to myself there are seven witnesses, including Karegeya Bunani's wife. Since this case has been delayed so many times, I have been given the impression that there are no other witnesses at all.

"Let's start, but first there are some rules that you will have to respect and follow," the President says. "First, whoever wants to speak, must request that by raising his hand. The President is the one and only one to give speeches. Second, whoever is speaking must aim at speaking the whole truth."

I have heard words to this effect for all the years I have attended *gacaca* court in my own community. So I barely listen.

"We seek to mete out justice," the President continues, "but also promote reconciliation so our country can move united into a better future."

I have heard these words, too, but question whether they are appropriate today. Most *gacaca* courts begin with a confession of a crime and an expression of remorse. Only then does the guilty one beg the community for forgiveness. Only then can reconciliation begin. But Karegeya Bunani has confessed nothing. He has shown no remorse or asked for any forgiveness. He has denied everything.

I have no interest in reconciliation with Bunani. For the President to even mention the word makes me wonder even before we start if I have come here for nothing.

I will not reconcile with that monster. I seek justice and nothing more. I crave it.

The President speaks my name, and I look up.

"Mutesi Bizimungu has the right for her testimony to be heard in a closed session," he says. "*Gacaca* trials have been based on open community participation, as you all know. But the revised *gacaca* laws of 2008 state that when testimony will be of such a graphic sexual and potentially shameful variety, the person may demand a closed session, and must be given one."

The crowd murmurs at this, and I feel my cheeks grow warm, but I hold my head high.

"I decline the offer of a closed session, Mr. President," I say. "I would like the world to know what was done to me, but since the United Nations has decided not to hear my voice, I wish this entire community to hear it. I demand that this entire community hear it."

The murmurs grow even louder, but the President ignores them.

"Okay, today we are dealing with the case of Karegeya Bunani," the President says. "I want to ask both sides, victims and suspects, you see the *gacaca* court in front of you. On the victim's side, is there any one that you do not trust? On the suspects' side?"

"I do not trust Mutesi Bizimungu," Bunani's wife says, pointing at me. "She is mentally imbalanced and a liar."

A clamor erupts, but above it a middle-aged woman

in red-and-black plaid robes and a matching headdress shouts, "I have heard that, too."

"I have as well," says another woman's voice who I can't even identify.

"Quiet!" the President snaps. "One at a time. And if you don't have anything more than unfounded rumors, please stay silent. If Mutesi Bizimungu is mentally unbalanced, we need to know what the evidence is of that. And if she is a liar, then on what basis do you say that?"

They are all silent for a moment, and then Bunani's wife says, "I know that what she says about my husband is a lie. And I also have heard that Mutesi Bizimungu claims to have been raped by all these men, but she does not have the HIV. That seems hard to believe. She is a liar!"

My ears burn and the clamor breaks into audible phrases.

"Got to be a liar!"

"Bunani is a good man!"

"No HIV!"

"*Quiet!*" the President all but shouts. "I will have no more of this! None of it!"

He glares at all those in attendance, and for once, I have faith that my words will be heard. The President is a man of principle.

"Okay now. We usually have the defendant speak first, especially if he is admitting his guilt and asking for forgiveness," the President says. "But in this case, Karegeya Bunani is claiming innocence, so we will ask Mutesi Bizimungu to step forward and tell us her story."

I step forward. Gasps erupt from the audience as I begin to describe the events at the church.

"Excuse me," the President interrupts, "but are you claiming Karegeya Bunani was involved in any of the events at the church?"

"I do not know," I say. "I was unconscious for part of the time."

"But you didn't see Karegeya Bunani at the church. Is that correct?"

I stare at the President. I am supposed to be able to tell my story. He may ask questions, as may any of the judges, but he is acting as though he is Bunani's lawyer, and lawyers are expressly forbidden in *gacaca*.

"No, I didn't see him at the church," I say. "He might have been there. He might not. The first I saw him was when he raped me in what he called his 'love hut.'"

"Then why don't you begin starting with *when you say* you first saw him," the President says, making the emphasis on "when you say" quite obvious. It's such a glaring move that the woman judge next to him in her bright yellow robes looks sharply at him, eyebrows raised. Even she is shocked.

I begin to wonder if Bunani has bought his acquittal. It is a problem with *gacaca*. The judges are elected, but they are not paid. The time investment is substantial so for a young man like the President who has not yet become financially secure, bribes can compensate for the unpaid work.

But I'm not giving up. I tell of Bunani's atrocities. I speak of what he did to me and of the unnamed friends he shared me with. I tell of his threats of gang rape to force my cooperation, threats that forced me to say that I loved him, threats that forced me to pretend that I enjoyed what he did to me.

"She liked it!" I hear someone utter in disgust amidst the gasps. And from another, "She loved him!"

When I am done, I look about me and see the disbelief in so many people's eyes. The President's next question gives voice to their thoughts.

"What evidence do you have to prove your claims?" he asks.

I hold out my hands. "You can see the scars on my wrists where the cuffs wore at the skin." I lift my full-length robes scant inches off the ground. "They are on my ankles as well."

I also hold out five papers from the hospital I was treated at after my rescue. "These are my hospital papers and they confirm what I have said. I am not mentally imbalanced." I glare for a moment at Bunani's wife. "I have been brutalized in a most unthinkable way."

I step forward and hand the papers to the President and show him and the rest of the judges my wrists. He passes the papers to the other judges.

"We see your evidence and we grieve for you," the President says. "But is there proof that it was Karegeya Bunani specifically who performed these shameful acts?"

"I had hoped that you or the other judges would have found additional evidence," I say. "But if not, you have my testimony."

Bunani steps forward and gives his testimony of all the appointments and public places where he was seen at the same time he was supposedly raping me.

Supposedly.

"Is this evidence complete and true?" the President asks.

I can only shake my head, since I have no right under *gacaca* to cross-examine Bunani. Instead, his wife and six other witnesses, two of them relatives and four employees in his fish markets, corroborate Bunani's testimony. The murmuring in the crowd grows with every word spoken that, in effect, calls me a liar.

"If that is all," the President says, "we will announce our findings next week."

I know already what those findings will be. It will scarcely be worth the effort for me to return here and hear words that will be like daggers to my heart. And so I stand up to speak one last time.

"May say one more thing, Mr. President?"

"You have already had your chance to speak, Mutesi Bizimungu." He looks at me with an air of sadness. "But you have travelled a long way and if your words are true, you have suffered great harm. So I will grant you a minute or two more."

I nod my thanks and begin.

"I have spoken of all that happened, and will repeat none of it now. But I must tell you that what was done to me follows me wherever I—"

"Mr. President!" Bunani says, leaping to his feet. "This woman has already spoken her lies. How much more will she be allowed to destroy my good name?"

The President nods. He is about to agree with Bunani. I am sure of it.

"Let her speak!" a woman calls out from off to my

right. She is wearing a traditional plaid orange-and-blue robe and matching headdress. She raises a hand to her mouth, appearing surprised at her own outburst. Fear is in her eyes.

Bunani stares at her. His eyes widen for an instant, then his outrage returns in even greater measure. "Mr. President!"

"*Silence!*" the President commands. He looks gravely all about him. "I have granted Mutesi Bizimungu no more than a minute or two. That is my ruling. She will be allowed to speak."

I nod and thank him. I hold my head high.

"Wherever I go," I say, "whether it is into the fields to toil the land or to the markets to buy food or even to my own hut to lay down and sleep, I always smell Karegeya Bunani. The foul odor of fish that was in his clothes and on his skin and in his hair never leaves me. That stench, and the smell of his semen, never leaves my nostrils—"

A cry erupts from the woman dressed in plaid orange-and-blue. "It's true! It's true!" She bows her head, and buries her face in one hand. "He raped me, too," she says, sobbing. She holds three fingers up and shakes her hand violently in the direction of Bunani. "Three times. Three times he raped me. The smell stays with me, too. Mostly at night when I try to sleep. I smell him as if he is lying there beside me."

She looks beside her, where a man stares at her in shock and disbelief. "I told no one, least of all my husband." She touches his arm and wipes tears off her cheeks. "He is a jealous man, and I thought he would want me no longer." She shakes her head. "I am sorry, but I can remain silent no more. Bunani is an evil man."

And then another cry erupts from off to my left. "She's right. He did it to me, too." This woman, short and squat, dressed in a Western style dark blue dress, points a finger at Bunani. "I felt such shame. I could tell no one. You stole my life away from me."

I turn to Bunani just in time to see his wife slap him hard across the face. Bunani topples backward, and his wife slaps him again.

"You better hope they throw you in jail," she says loud enough for all to hear, "because if they do not, I will kill you myself."

———

WITH KAREGEYA BUNANI in the jail cell he so richly deserves, my thoughts turn from justice to escaping the shackles of my memories. Perhaps those chains will bind me and the two women who stood for me in the *gacaca* court until our very last breath.

But I choose to believe that we will one day break free. I cling to that hope. We will escape from that bondage. And yet never, ever forget.

HURAM'S TEMPLE

INTRODUCTION TO HURAM'S
TEMPLE

O riginally, I wasn't going to include this story. It's the only one that has previously appeared in one of my other collections (*Death in the Serengeti and Other Stories: Ten Tales of Crime*), and I already had sufficient stories and words for this one.

But if you're collecting crime stories from other eras and you have one that goes all the way back to Old Testament Israel (and one originally published in the revered pages of *Ellery Queen's Mystery Magazine*), then only a fool would leave it out.

So here it is.

By the way, if "Old Testament Israel" stopped you dead in your tracks and you're tempted to skip to the next story, let me use the same words of reassurance I wrote years ago in that previous collection.

Trust me, there will be no theology. Only murder.

HURAM'S TEMPLE

I OFTEN WONDER whether the foundry we work in belongs to Huram, the Phoenician, or King Solomon. It was, of course, the king who ordered and paid for its construction, from the furnace and casting pits to the metalworking tools and benches to the stores of copper and tin. It may be the largest bronze foundry in all the world, over fifty paces by fifty paces in size, filled with over a dozen artisans and twenty slaves. The king built it to furnish his great temple with treasures.

But Huram acts as though it is his very own. A man of prodigious girth and self-love, he struts about, issuing orders both to the men he brought with him from Tyre and true Israelites alike. As if no one else has so much as cast a single medal before in our lives. He is the master artist; we are nothing.

"No!" Huram bellows at one of his men. "You've lost the detail! Start all over. Do it again."

I glance at my friend Elam. We exchange knowing looks and his ruddy face glows, and not just from the sweat caused by the blasting heat of the furnace, stoked hot enough to turn the copper and tin molten. Elam's jovial face always glows with an inner radiance, as if all things amuse him. But in this case he has an extra reason to be merry. We have a wager on how often Huram will explode in anger today, and Elam has just taken one step closer to winning.

My eyes turn to Elam's father, Abimael, but he looks angrily away as if telling us to mind our business. Abimael. Ever serious. Ever bowing to the genius of Huram of Tyre. The three of us are the lone Israelites isolated in a den of Phoenicians and their slaves, but Elam and I often feel as separated from his father as if he, too, worships Baal instead of Jehovah, the god of King Solomon and all true Israelites.

The Phoenicians deny the sacrilege, of course, not wanting to spit on the coins given to them by the king for their labors. They say they believe in many gods, including Jehovah, but is that not forbidden by the tablets Moses brought down from the mount, tablets still resting in the Ark of the Covenant? When the temple is complete and it houses the Ark, will not those tablets cry out at the sacrilege of being surrounded by treasures designed by impure hands?

May King Solomon reign a thousand years and ten. But how could he choose a man from Tyre instead of a true Israelite as his master sculptor? Even if his genius towers over all of us. True, Huram's mother is a widow from the tribe of Naphtali, but his father is a Phoenician craftsman. Huram is a man of Tyre, not Jerusalem. How can the works of an uncircumcised man share a temple with the great Ark of the Covenant?

Within the foundry, he acts as if he is a pagan god himself.

"No, fool!" he shouts at another Phoenician. "You've ruined it again!"

Huram rarely shouts at the three of us Israelites, but that's only because he assigns all the most difficult work, all the most interesting pieces, to his own men while treating us as if we have no skills at all. Our stature ranks barely higher than that of the slaves.

All about me, men use their tools, chipping away the molds surrounding hardened casts or adding fine details to the bronze itself. The clanging of the tools fills my ears. Pieces of the molds crash to the ground as they are broken away from the casts. The slaves stoke the furnace. The smell of its intense fire is in the air.

I press soft wax against my mold so it will capture every detail for the bowl I am working on. In my design, a thread winds around and around and then spins off to start another thread that winds its way all the way around the outside of the bowl. An interesting design, but...

The Phoenicians prepare molds for lions and oxen and cherubim. Mine are for bowls.

Sweat pours down my face, dripping off my chin onto my garments, even as my righteous anger remains bottled inside with no avenue of escape. With a rag, I wipe my face and dry my wet hair, though I wonder why. There is no point. The furnace at the center of the foundry radiates heat of such force that every one of us drips sweat all day. The place reeks of it.

Elam is about to pour molten bronze into his mold when the clatter of hoofs sounds outside. As if in unison, we all turn to the entrance, free men and slaves alike. The room, moments before filled with loud clanging, falls silent. It has been days since the last rain; stirred-up dust that makes its way inside will ruin our work.

"Go away!" Huram shouts as he strides toward the entrance, an angry glare on his face. "I command it!"

The clatter of hoofs slows to a halt. Outside, men dismount and trumpets sound. Two voices, one higher than the other, call out, "Make way for Joakim, envoy of the great King Solomon, may he reign a thousand years and ten!"

I set down my mold. What can this mean? I glance at Elam and Abimael, eyebrows raised but receive only shrugs in return. The three of us and the Phoenicians file out. The slaves, looking even more confused than the rest of us, begin to join us until Huram sees them.

"Tend the furnace!" he commands, and struts out ahead of us into the open clearing that surrounds the foundry. A hundred paces to the north, a long row of tents begins and stretches outward. A hundred paces to the east lies the storehouse where the finished objects are kept.

A cooling breeze wafts over our wet skin. I run my fingers through my damp hair and let the air flow over me like cleansing water. Elam sees me and grins.

"Feels good, doesn't it?" he asks softly.

"Be quiet!" Abimael says through clenched teeth.

Two men standing beside sleek black horses hold ceremonial horns at their sides, their attention directed toward a man seated on a carriage drawn by two pale white horses. Joakim, no doubt. Almost as rotund as Huram, Joakim is clad in royal colors and possesses a fair countenance. Following in his wake are six donkeys, all loaded down with large, coarse sacks. When he's drawn to within thirty paces, he commands his driver to stop. He stands.

Dust billows. The odors of the animals carry downwind to me; I'm not the only one to notice. Elam grimaces in comic overreaction and his father hisses at us both.

Joakim clears his throat and puffs out his chest. "I send greetings from the great King Solomon," he says. "He anxiously awaits the fruits of your labor. They shall make his temple beyond compare."

Joakim smiles at us. I wonder if we are supposed to cheer.

"The king has spared no expense," he continues, "summoning the great master Huram from the land of Tyre."

Huram puffs out his chest and smiles smugly. I want to strike him. Even Abimael looks annoyed.

Joakim points to the donkeys. "The king sends more copper and tin aboard these beasts of burden so that the greatness of his temple shall know no bounds. Your toil shall fill it with treasures such as his people have never seen."

He pauses, seeming to wait for cheers, forgetting that almost of his audience are Phoenicians. Not King Solomon's people. Not Joakim's people. For that matter, not Jehovah's people.

"Are you Huram of Tyre?" Joakim asks, gesturing in

Huram's direction. "Are you the man who will show me the king's treasures?"

I wonder how he made the correct guess. Do the rich and powerful smell better than the rest of us? I would surely hope so. Or is it just the wide girth of those with the means to eat more than just their daily bread?

"Yes, I am Huram." The smug look returns to his face. Surprising us all, he bows. "At the king's service with what talents I may possess."

What talents I may possess. Like Esau of old and his hunger for a bowl of porridge, I would forfeit my birthright, if I had one, for the chance to slap this arrogant man. Such is my hunger.

"Then you shall lead me to the storehouse where the completed pieces have been collected," Joakim says. "I shall inspect them to see that the king will not be disappointed."

"He will not be disappointed," Huram says. "You may be certain of that. You know of my talents and I've brought with me the most renowned bronze-working artisans from the great city of Tyre. Our work shall please the king, of that I am sure."

The most renowned bronze-working artisans from the great city of Tyre. While the Phoenicians look on in pride, I try to recall who he might have omitted. Hmm. I wonder. Abimael's lips are pursed so tightly they are turning white. I want to spit on the ground. Elam himself looks on with heavy-lidded eyes, not seeming to care about the insult. Content, even when he has no right to be.

I now have another subject I'd like to slap.

THREE GUARDS STAND outside the storehouse, their spears sharp and their shields bearing the king's seal. Because of that seal, the treasures destined for the temple are safe within the storehouse; a man who violates that seal forfeits his life.

The guards move aside and Joakim and Huram step forward. Everyone else gathers around along the two walls closest to the entrance.

The larger pieces are arrayed on thick wood planking, protecting them from ground moisture; the smaller ones rest on solid wood tables. Smooth cloths cover each one, concealing them from view.

Huram strides to the nearest table and faces Joakim.

"These will decorate the temple's front pillars when they are completed," Huram says. With a flourish, he yanks off the cloth.

Fifty brass pomegranates cover the table, the red-gold shimmering of the bronze making it look like gold itself.

Joakim draws in his breath sharply. He moves to within a hand's breadth to examine them more closely.

"What detail!" Joakim exclaims. "The fruit looks like it is about to burst open."

Huram steps to the next table. "These also will decorate the pillars."

He pulls aside the cloth to display four linked chains of bronze curling back on each other, each one extending over thirty paces long.

Joakim nods his approval.

Huram skips past the tables he once derisively

referred to as "the Israelite section" and moves to a large form resting on the planking. He yanks off the cloth.

An immense bronze ox stares at the king's envoy, its black eyes lifelike, its great tail in the midst of swatting away invisible flies.

Joakim continues his praise.

Huram moves through the other major pieces, giving special attention to a lion with a most lifelike mane, until only two remain. He stands before a cloth covering a piece that rises to his chest. The room seems to hold its collective breath. Even I await the verdict.

Huram delicately removes the cloth, displaying a bronze water lily almost four feet tall, its petals and stem a work of art, one that I concede is far beyond my abilities or Elam's of Abimael's and will always be so.

Joakim's face flushes as if besotted by a beautiful woman. "It's magnificent!" He examines the fine detail, the way the stems bend in such a lifelike fashion. "King Solomon will be amazed."

Huram beams. He waits for Joakim to recover before they move on.

"And the final piece," Huram says, his voice shaking with excitement as he pulls aside the cloth. "The cherubim."

The work depicts five of them, each with wings unfurled and cheeks glowing with the bronze's red-gold shimmer. Their hands meet in the middle where in King Solomon's temple, they will hold a candle with their finely detailed fingers.

Joakim gasps. He cannot speak. A hand moves to his mouth.

"This work is extraordinary," he says finally. "The king..." He shakes his head. "Just extraordinary. Huram, you are a master. And your men are artisans of the highest order."

Joakim surveys the room. "Is everyone here?" he asks, then looks at Huram. "Except for the slaves, of course."

Huram counts us to be sure. He nods. "Yes."

"Tonight," Joakim says, "we shall have a feast of celebration for I will be bringing the king the greatest of reports. His temple will be a great wonder, the most splendid to be found." He spreads his hands wide. "Tonight we shall kill the fatted calf and drink the king's wine."

The room erupts in cheers. Elam pounds his hands together. Even grim Abimael allows himself a smile.

Joakim holds up his hand for silence.

"I am also authorized to grant each man a bonus of five shekels payable on the morrow." The cheering erupts even louder. He leans toward Huram and whispers something. Huram nods and smiles.

I wonder at the size of Huram's bonus, surely their topic of discussion, until Elam claps me on the shoulder.

"I told you they'd take care of us," he says.

"The Lord provides for his people," Abimael says.

"Now you can stop being so cynical," Elam says, that jovial face of his beaming even more broadly. "Tonight we shall drink of the king's wine, partake of the fatted calf, and roll the dice to separate the Phoenicians from their shekels."

Even as Abimael frowns, I feel my spirits soar.

Now *that* will be a fitting end to the evening.

ELAM AND I eat and drink until the night is late, as do all the men from Tyre, even the master himself, Huram, who partakes enough of the fatted calf to expand his girth in just the one meal. We sing merry songs that grow more bawdy by the hour, even joining in with the Phoenicians.

Only Abimael retires early, the merriment too much for his disposition, a feisty psalm about all he can handle.

Joakim drinks little, choosing instead to send his portions to Elam and me, which we gratefully accept. I've never known my friend to decline a skin of wine.

Elam and I take on the Phoenicians in some rolls of the dice, but sadly it is they who separate us from our shekels and not the other way around.

When we have lost all our money and drank all the wine, Elam and I stagger back to his father's tent, commiserating in our losses, certain the Phoenicians cheated but unsure how. We're drunk enough that we can barely say the words, much less figure out how we lost.

We enter the tent and collapse onto the ground, knowing the morning will come all too soon.

BUT IT ISN'T MORNING. The night is still dark and Abimael is shaking us both awake.

"Do you hear that?" he whispers urgently.

I rub my eyes. My stomach roils. From the other side of the tent, I hear Elam groan.

"Listen!" Abimael says.

I lift my head but hear nothing.

"They're just having fun," I say, my speech slurred.

"No, not that way. Over there." Abimael points toward the storehouse. "Come with me."

But I can't clear my head. I actually make it onto all fours but then topple over.

"You two!" Abimael says in disgust and then leaves.

An instant before I fall back asleep, I hear Elam snore.

"*WHERE IS ABIMAEL*?" a deep, angry voice bellows.

I lift my head off the ground and groan. The harsh words echo painfully in my head; bright sunlight pierces my eyes. Several paces away, Elam moans, sounding as bad as I feel.

I make out two of the largest Phoenicians, ugly and imposing, glaring at us from the mouth of the tent.

"Where is Abimael?" says the larger of the two. An old scar runs along his eyebrow.

I push myself up on one elbow. Everything spins until I close my eyes. I open them and try to focus on the spot where Abimael should be lying. He's not there.

The Phoenician with the scar turns toward the storehouse and yells, "It is the Israelites! It is Abimael!"

The two men drag us roughly to our feet and haul us outside. I try to clear my mind even as my stomach roils. I vaguely recall Abimael waking us in the middle of the night and saying something about the storehouse. But what?

"Bring me the Israelites!" a voice bellows from over by the storehouse. Huram.

Elam and I stare at each other. Elam's eyes widen.

"I shall have their heads!" Huram continues.

As the two Phoenicians drag us toward the storehouse, others rush at us from every direction, quickly surrounding us, fury in their eyes. The one with the scar says, "They would steal the treasures from their own temple!" He spits on the ground before our feet.

Elam looks at me with alarm. After so many years of seeing that ruddy face without a care in the world, that look chills me. Far more than the spit of an ugly Phoenician.

"Where is my father?" Elam says, his voice filled with fear.

"Where indeed," the scarred Phoenician says.

The rest of the camp, save the slaves, is gathered at the storehouse. The three daytime guards stand before the entrance even though their watch is not yet due. Though day has broken, this is still the hour for the night watch.

As he sees us come nigh, Huram's face turns almost purple with rage. "What have you done with them?" Behind Huram, Joakim glares.

"Done with what?" I ask.

"My treasures," Huram says. "The two prize pieces. The cherubim and the water lilies. They are my greatest works. I must have them back!"

"The *king*," Joakim says with cold fire in his voice, "must have them back."

A pang of regret passes over Huram's face, and then he nods. "Yes, the *king* must have them back."

"We know not of what you speak," I say, knowing that no matter what the answer, it bodes ill for us.

"Where is my father?" Elam says.

"We have searched the entire camp," Joakim says coldly. "Every Phoenician and every slave is accounted for. Only Abimael is missing. The reason is clear. In the dead of night, he stole the treasures and fled." Joakim's eyes narrow. "After killing the king's three guards."

My jaw drops. To be accused by Huram or any of his men is a fearsome enough thing; we are but three amidst a den of vile Phoenicians. But for a fellow Israelite, a representative of the great King Solomon, to make the charge turns me cold.

"Do not pretend that you do not know," Joakim says.

"Why do you speak ill of my father?" Elam says. "He has never stolen so much as a shekel in his life. He is the most honest man I know."

"Then why is he, and he alone, missing?" Joakim asks.

I recall now Abimael asking us to join him, then leaving without us for the storehouse, but I can scarcely admit that. Those words would condemn him further still. I look to Elam, who stares helplessly back.

"The thief is missing," Huram thunders, "because he has fled with the cherubim and water lilies. Why else?" He points at us, as he has so often in the past, though then only to sneer. Now it means our lives. "The Israelites are not like us." He looks at Joakim, realizes that he, too, is an Israelite, and flushes. "The three of them share their own tent. They share their own counsel, eating and working together, apart from my men. They hold back no secrets from each other. These two know where Abimael is. They must. They will lead us to the treasures."

"Guards," Joakim says to the three guards. "Seize these two men."

The lead guard, a man with whom I shared a riddle but three days ago, and two others, one on each side, stand before Elam and me, their spears ready.

In a trembling voice, Elam asks, "What have you done with my father?"

I try to piece it together. Who could have stolen the cherubim and water lilies? Where are they now? What happened and when? And where is Abimael? What did he do after he left our tent? And why does Joakim suspect an Israelite over so many men of Tyre?

Some of the answers, one in particular, I fear I already know. My mind, lost in a fog just minutes ago but now clear as a bright summer day, races but not fast enough.

"I must depart to report to the king," Joakim says. "My men are preparing the animals now."

The Phoenicians begin to murmur, glancing angrily amongst themselves. The word "shekels" can clearly be heard. They care only of their own greed, not of the lives of Israelites. I wonder which of them has committed this treachery.

Joakim glares at them. "I will pay your shekels upon my return so long as the stolen treasures are found," he says. "Surely you do not expect the king to pay a bonus when the most prized treasures are missing."

The Phoenicians fall silent and stare at the ground as the King's carriage, drawn by the two white horses, arrives. The driver turns it around and waits. Over a hundred paces away, Joakim's two men are on their black horses leading away the beasts of burden. Two of the donkeys appear so lame I wonder if they'll survive the trip back to Jerusalem.

"Must you tell the king about the theft?" Huram asks. He licks his lips. "A king's anger is a hard thing to suffer. Many treasures remain. Almost all of them, in fact. The great ox. The lion. The pomegranates and chain links for the pillars. We will find the thief Abimael. The treasures will come back to the storehouse."

"And if you fail?" Joakim asks. "If you never see the treasures again?"

Huram looks as though he's been told of the death of his firstborn. My hatred of the man almost distracts me into pleasure at his agony. "I will get them back," he says. "I *must* get them back." His jaw sets. "And if not, then we shall make others that are their equal. I swear it."

"And what of the death of the guards?"

Huram blinks. His obsession over his lost treasures has blinded him to the deaths of the three men. And almost certainly, I think, a fourth.

"The slaves will bury them," he says. "I will send word to their families."

"But the king must send replacements bearing his seal."

Huram's shoulders slump. "That is true."

"The king must be told of the guards," Joakim says. "But I will spare you the king's wrath over the lost treasures, so long as the next time I arrive, they have been replaced."

With sudden clarity, I see it all inside my head. What happened. What I must do.

I step forward, fury welling up within me.

"I can tell you where the treasures are," I say.

Joakim looks startled.

"Where are my cherubim and water lilies?" Huram says. "You know where Abimael has taken them?"

"I know not of Abimael, though I have my fears," I say. I clench my fists in rage.

"This man speaks in riddles," Joakim says. "Guard, take him away!"

I glare at Joakim, hating him more now than Huram and all his Phoenicians combined. "The bronze cherubim and water lilies ride aboard this man's donkeys," I say. "The two that are near to collapsing from the weight." I point to where Joakim's men are leading the beasts of burden away.

Joakim strikes me across the face. "How dare you insult me, envoy of the great King Solomon?"

I resist the urge to strike him back. He is the king's representative, though for but a few moments more if I am right.

"Prove me wrong," I say, knowing my life weighs in the balance, if it is not already forfeit. "Tell your men to return here."

"I'll not take orders from a prisoner!"

I turn to the guards. "This man killed your three comrades. Will you protect him now?"

"I'll listen to this no more," Joakim says, his voice quivering.

He goes to board the carriage, but Huram grabs his arm. "Did you steal my water lilies? The cherubim?"

The guard I shared the riddle with blocks Joakim's way. "If you killed my comrades, you broke the king's seal and will be condemned to death. We will go to your animals. If the treasures are not there, the prisoner dies. But if the prisoner is right—"

"Stop this madness!" Joakim says, but the guards continue to block his way.

In little time, we overtake Joakim's men. Their horses could outrace us, but the heavily burdened donkeys cannot.

The lead guard moves close to the first beast. It arrived to the foundry with a large, coarse sack strapped atop its back, the sack loaded with copper or tin for smelting. Now, the sack remains filled to overflowing, as does the one other. Two donkeys are carrying heavy sacks; the others, nothing.

I hold my breath as the guard slashes the sack. At first, only sand pours out, and I feel my own life departing with it. But then the wondrous red-gold shimmer of bronze appears.

Huram stumbles over to protect the piece from falling. He guides it out safely, like a midwife with a newborn, and holds the brass cherubim in his trembling hands.

"When Joakim saw the cherubim and the lilies," I say, "he had to possess them. He could not share them with all the people of Israel. Such was his greed. They had to be his own.

"He offered shekels he would never have to pay so that we would celebrate, then got us drunk so that only the three guards would stand between him and the treasures, guards who would naturally show deference to the king's envoy and be easily slain with the help of his two men."

I look about. Every eye is either on me or is shifting to Joakim with a look of disbelief.

"One more man, however, stood between him and the treasures," I say. "Abimael, the one man who did not partake beyond what thirst required of the king's wine. And when he left his tent for the storehouse and discovered Joakim's treachery, he paid for it with his life."

All eyes now are on Joakim, who stands silent and unwavering, lips pursed.

"Where did you bury him?" Elam asks, tears streaming down his dirt-streaked face.

Joakim's men leap aboard their horses and try to race off, but the Phoenicians yank them down and throw them to the ground. Joakim stares straight ahead.

I look to Huram, whose guilt I had so desired but been denied. "Why would Joakim conceal the theft from the king if not to insure the safety of the treasures in his own hands? Did you think he would risk his life as a favor to you?" I spare the vain man no more than I've spared Joakim. "Not every man loves you, Huram, as much as you love yourself."

Huram winces. After a time, he points to the sack strapped to the other donkey. Once again, the guard uses his spear and cuts open the sack. Sand pours out until the bronze water lily slowly appears.

It is broken in two, its delicate stem severed.

A wail escapes from Huram's lips. He grabs the nearest guard's spear. I guess that the guard knows what is about to happen but has allowed the weapon to slip through his hands.

Huram leans back and plunges the spear into Joakim's chest.

Joakim gasps. His eyes grow pleasurably wide. He drops to his knees, grasping at the spear even as the ground about him turns dark red.

Death comes fast.

But not with nearly enough pain.

HOUSEWARMING GIFT

INTRODUCTION TO
HOUSEWARMING GIFT

Here we are back in the sixties. My wheelhouse. And in Greater Boston, no less. My hometown.

So why did I choose to write about Boston's overt racism of that era? What about hometown loyalty?

Sometimes when an issue seizes you, you're left with no choice. Hometown or not.

I didn't *choose* to write "Housewarming Gift." I felt *compelled* to write it. I felt *compelled* to examine and expose the story's undeniable and uncomfortable truth.

Fortunately, one aspect of that truth made it an ideal fit for the *Mystery, Crime, and Mayhem* issue titled *Sins of the Fathers*.

HOUSEWARMING GIFT

G arrett Harrison didn't notice that the front door was slightly ajar until he went to unlock it. His heart skipped a beat, and his brown eyes widened.

Behind him on the lighted porch stood his wife Bea and his two daughters, Marie, who was twelve, and Janice, eight, all of them huddled against the cold in their black winter coats, matching woolen scarfs looped around their necks, and hats covering their Afros. Temperatures had dropped into the teens as darkness had fallen on this Friday evening, and a stiff wind made it feel colder still even as it carried the slight, but pleasing scent of the snow-covered rose bushes that lined the ranch-style house. Garrett, who would soon turn forty and stood not quite six feet tall and weighed one seventy-five, loved those rose bushes. They had been the first thing that had attracted both Bea and him to the house, which they'd moved into just two weeks ago.

But as Garrett stared at the door left ajar, he wasn't thinking about the rose bushes or the thick, green lawn, covered now by a foot of snow, or the well-regarded school system in this upper middle class suburb north of Boston. He was thinking about how the neighbors had banded together and attempted to outbid him for the house, determined to keep the neighborhood lily white, desperate to keep him and his family out.

"It's an Irish Catholic neighborhood and town," the bald, pudgy realtor had explained, then earned his place in the hottest parts of Hell when he blithely added, "They're just trying to preserve its character and charm. And to be totally honest, they're also trying to preserve their property values. You should really look elsewhere, Mr. Harrison."

No, Garrett and his family were not going to look elsewhere. They weren't going to be bullied out of the home they'd fallen in love with. After all, this was suburban Massachusetts, not Mississippi. And it was 1968, not 1948. Richard Nixon may have just been elected President of the United States—unfortunately, in Garrett's opinion—but at least it hadn't been the Alabama segregationist, George Wallace.

No cross had been burned on their front lawn. At least, not yet.

Garrett hadn't worked his fingers to the bone, first toiling at a downtown Boston newsstand as a teenager and saving every last cent, then buying that newsstand, and then another and another until after over two decades of pinching every penny until it hurt, he could finally buy his family the house of their dreams. Not lavish or opulent. But a beautiful ranch-style house in the suburbs in which the girls each had a bedroom of their own, and where the streets were clean, the lawns thick green (except when covered with bright, white snow), and the schools excellent, especially compared to the ones in the black neighborhoods that the Boston school committee deliberately underfunded compared to those in the white neighborhoods.

Being able to buy this house for his family had been one of Garrett's proudest moments. His chest swelled at the very thought of it.

This was success. *This* made the long hours and the pinched pennies worth it. No amount of cold, unfriendly stares from the neighbors or the outright hostility of extended middle fingers or the racial epithets shouted from passing cars or even the dark-haired, rail-thin eighteen-year-old who'd drawn his finger across his throat, none of that could rob Garrett of his joy and satisfaction at owning this house.

Although it did make him wonder, his heart turning as frozen as his fingers, if all of that raw hatred was connected to the slightly ajar front door.

"Hurry, Daddy, I'm cold," Janice said, stomping her feet not in a temper tantrum but clearly in an effort to warm her thin, brown legs, uncovered by either her dress or coat.

"Bea, take the girls to the car," Garrett said in as flat a voice as he could manage with his heart pounding. He held out the keys.

"What's the problem?" Bea asked, an edge in her voice.

"Front door isn't shut tight. And I'm sure I slammed it and locked it before we went out."

They'd gone to Sears Roebuck for one last round of Christmas shopping, the girls having pointed out their fondest wishes in the thick Sears Wishbook Christmas catalog as well as its companion Toys catalog, each of them over six hundred pages. Most of the girls' gifts were already wrapped and under the tree. But the last batch— "the icing on the cake" in Bea's words—were back in the trunk of the car to be brought into the house away from Marie and Janice's prying eyes once they were up in their bedrooms. To maximize the fun and suspense, Garrett and Bea had made a big production out of making the purchases away from the girls and then Garrett bringing them out to the car while Bea rode the escalators with the girls even as Marie protested that she was far too old for such a baby distraction.

Garrett pointed to the doorjamb. Though its dark brown stain matched the color of the door exactly, the ajar nature of the door was unmistakable even in the darkness broken only by the light directly overhead.

Bea gasped. "Oh, no!" Her shoulders slumped, and a tired look came over her beautiful brown face. Tired, and almost defeated. She visibly swallowed and licked her lips.

"Girls, get behind me," Bea said, ignoring Garrett's offered keychain and extending her arms out to shepherd the girls back. "Garrett, should we call the police?"

Garrett gave her the what-kind-of-fool-are-you look that he knew she hated, but he couldn't help himself. First off, the phone was *inside*. And there were no friendly neighbors they could just waltz over to and ask to use theirs. Even more importantly, the town police had followed the Harrisons' car almost every day for the first week and had even pulled Garrett over and searched him the first day.

"Sorry, dumb idea," Bea said. "But I don't like the idea of you going in there alone while we sit in the car and don't know what's going on."

"Then at least get the girls in the car," Garrett said, then when Bea didn't instantly respond, he bypassed her and handed the keys to Marie, the older of the two girls. "Marie, take your sister to the car, get inside, and lock it. Don't open it for anyone but your mother and me." He winced. "Or the police."

A troubled, fearful look came over Marie's pretty brown eyes. The joyful exuberance in them just five minutes ago was long gone. Her voice trembled. "What's wrong?"

"I'm sure nothing," Garrett said. "We're just being extra cautious. Now go along back to the car." He was about to scold, "Don't make me tell you again," but realized gentleness was called for now, so he smiled. "Be the good big sister." He winked. "And don't you dare open the trunk."

The girls made their way back to the car, looking back over their shoulders multiple times, then climbed into the back bench seat inside the year-old, silver Plymouth Fury, Janice first and then Marie.

"I'll get a knife in the kitchen and check every room in the house," Garrett said to Bea. "I don't want either you or the girls stepping inside until I'm sure it's safe. You wait here on the porch until I get back."

"Garrett—"

"If I'm not back in seven minutes, run to the car and get the three of you out of here."

"*Garrett!*"

"I'm sure it's nothing," he said, not believing that for an instant.

IT WASN'T NOTHING. It was awful. Worse than awful.

Garrett turned on the lights by the door and gasped. Spray-painted in big, black letters on the facing wall of the front room, directly above the turntable and hi-fi stereo receiver that rested atop a home entertainment center that housed over three hundred jazz, pop, and R&B albums, was one word.

NIGGA.

A framed black-and-white photograph on the wall of the late Dr. Martin Luther King had been shattered, as had been a family portrait. The sofa below the front picture window was unscathed as was the TV on the other side of the entrance to the kitchen from the entertainment center.

In the far corner, however, to the right of the TV, the Christmas tree had been toppled over, several bulbs broken as well as the angel that had rested atop the tip of the tree. Presents had been hurled against the walls, and a few of them stomped on.

It looked like a bomb had gone off. Not literally, but almost. Only one present remained beside the toppled red tree stand. And the room smelled foul, the tree's spruce scent no longer the dominant, pleasing scent. Overwhelmed by some awful stench.

Garrett felt as though he'd been sucker-punched in the gut. His legs buckled and the room momentarily swayed in his vision.

Who would do something like this?

Of course, he knew the answer to that question. The candidates were countless. Hate and evil were in no short supply. He hadn't needed Dr. King's assassination eight months ago to educate him of that fact. He'd been living it his whole life.

Garrett narrowed his eyes and got into a crouch. Cautiously, he made his way to the kitchen, just beyond the front room. He flicked on the lights.

No one there.

Off the back of the counter beside the four-burner range—a top of the line Jenn-Aire—he grabbed the longest, sharpest knife they owned, the one he used to carve the Thanksgiving turkey, its serrated blade eight inches long.

Then, and only then, did he fully take in the same, shameful word spray-painted on the varnished pine cabinets.

That one word of pure hatred assaulted him on the walls of every room. The master bedroom and the girls' two bedrooms. Only the dining room had been spared and that had been because the word had been spray-painted *on* the dining room table, what had been an attractive dark wood surface, expandable to seat eight.

Not even the basement had been spared. The word

had been spray-painted on the concrete wall next to the furnace.

NIGGA.

The covers of all three beds had been pulled back and, based on the smell and the yellow stains on the white sheets in his and Bea's bed and the colorful pink sheets in Marie and Janice's, their intruder—their violator!—had urinated on all three beds.

A bitter taste flooded Garrett's mouth. His hands shook with rage.

So this was what the better life in the suburbs was all about? This was what his hard work had gotten him?

From the damp chill of the basement, he heard Bea's voice over the hum of the furnace, frantically calling his name.

Garrett! Garrett!!! Are you all right? Answer me!

Hollering back that he was safe, he bounded up the stairs two at a time, and raced to the front door, still gripping the serrated knife so hard it was a wonder the handle didn't shatter.

He dropped the knife when he neared Bea, who was standing in the doorway, eyes wide and frantic, tears streaming down her beautiful, brown face. Garrett wrapped his arms around her thin frame, holding her so tight he was afraid he might crack one of her ribs.

They squeezed each other tighter and tighter, and seemed to have a contest as to whom was shaking the harder, him from rage and her either from fear or rage or both.

Because she had clearly seen the one-word greeting

as soon as she'd opened the door and begun frantically calling her name.

"Just here?" Bea asked tearfully into his shoulder. "Or the whole house?"

"The whole house," Garrett said. "The whole damned house." And they held onto each other even more tightly.

Finally, Garrett pulled away, his heart still jackhammering, his breaths coming in huge, angry gulps.

"Let's get the girls," Garrett said, swallowing the lump in his throat.

"They shouldn't see this," Bea said, shaking her head, the tears pooled in her eyes continuing to spill down her cheeks.

Garrett brushed them away with as much softness as he could muster. "They have to. We can see if they can stay at your mother's tonight, or maybe even the three of you stay at a hotel, but this is going to take time to clean up." He pursed his lips and shook his head. "And there's no hiding this from them. They need to know."

Bea fetched the girls, both of whom were crying even before they saw their mother's tears. They stepped inside the house, and Garrett prepared to give the three women in his life the worst tour he could ever imagine.

But before they even got out of the front room and its toppled Christmas tree and the ruin of destroyed presents, sweet little Janice found the ultimate indignity. And the source of the stench.

With her black winter coat unbuttoned and her black woolen hat in her right hand, she frowned and walked to the fallen Christmas tree, an eight-foot-tall spruce back when it was still erect and held in place by the green metal, three-legged stand and it's red, water-filled bowl.

Janice stood over the one present that hadn't been stomped on or hurled against the walls. It was wrapped in green-and-red striped paper, and was shoebox-sized because inside were some patent leather dress shoes that she had begged for.

She picked up the box.

Garrett had just been about to shout a warning to leave it alone. It could have been left as a booby trap set to go off, but he'd been thinking about *that word* on the wall above the stereo, and how he was going to have to show it to his family so many more times. Not to mention the beds that had been urinated on, although perhaps the girls should be spared that. So he was too late to stop her. The words were still in his mouth when she picked up the present.

Janice screamed. She flung the box off to one side and raced back to her mother. She buried her face in Bea's side.

Garrett held back the urge to vomit. He clenched and unclenched his fists.

On the light blue, thick shag rug, beside the fallen tree and its sprinkled-loose needles, their violator had taken a shit.

———

THE KNOCK on their front door by the police came scant minutes after Garrett placed the call. He opened the door to two uniformed policemen standing beneath the porch light, one broad shouldered and about six feet tall, perhaps in his thirties with blond hair poking out from beneath his cap, and the other several inches shorter and more squat, more likely in his fifties.

The older, squat patrolman took the lead. "We'd like to speak to Mr. Harrison."

"That's me. I'm Garrett Harrison." And before he could stop himself, not sure he even wanted to stop considering his righteous rage, he added, "I'm not the butler. I'm the owner of this house."

"Yes, of course." The patrolman nodded. "You're the one."

"The one?" Garrett cocked his head. He knew he shouldn't get trapped in this game, but the turd left for them under the tree, and still there for the police to take note of, had scrambled his mind just a bit.

"The one who called in the complaint, of course," the cop said.

Which was not at all what he had meant, Garrett was sure. *The one* had meant the black family. The invaders who were ruining the "character of the neighborhood" and property values to boot.

The cop flashed a frozen smile. As if he hadn't known all along that this was the house of the black family with the car in the driveway that had been followed incessantly since they'd put the offer on the house.

The cop knew. And Garrett knew he knew. It was all just a charade.

"Come inside." Garrett said.

Garrett pointed out the spray-painted message on the front room wall, the destroyed Christmas presents, the toppled tree, and of course, the turd.

The exclamation point to the whole act.

Their special housewarming gift.

Welcome to the neighborhood!

The two cops nodded, but curiously, Garrett thought, took no notes. Or maybe that wasn't so curious at all.

He led them into the kitchen, pointed to the spray-painted message there, and to the dining room, where Bea had engaged the two girls in a game of Monopoly to try to get their minds off what had happened and bide time until the police were done investigating and she could strip all the beds. Bea had put down a tablecloth to cover the message on the table, but offered to pull it back to show the patrolmen.

They declined.

Garrett took the cops through the rest of the house. And found himself again clenching and unclenching his fists at not only the acts that had defiled their dream house—that had torn Garrett's heart and soul out! —but also the cops' barely disguised disinterest.

"You smell the urine?" Garrett asked as he pointed to Janice's bed. "Whoever did this pissed all over an eight-year-old's bed."

"Probably some kids," the lead cop said.

"Teenagers," the other one echoed.

"Probably not from here," the lead cop said.

"Maybe from Revere or Saugus or Lynn," the other added.

Breathing loudly through his nose, Garrett escorted them back to the front door.

"So what happens now?" he asked.

"We'll fill out the forms," the squat, older lead cop said. "You can contact your insurance company."

"And then what?"

"I guess they pay you whatever it costs to tidy things back up again," the lead cop said. "Minus the deductible, of course."

"What about you, though?" Garrett demanded. "What kind of investigation will *you* be doing?

The cop narrowed his eyes. "What kind of investigation do you think we'll be doing?"

Garrett felt the bitter, increasingly familiar taste in his mouth again. "Not a damned thing."

The cop gave a curt nod.

"What do you expect?" he said. "You've made yourself a target. You don't belong here. I know it. You know it. The whole world knows it. The sooner you fess up to that truth, the better." He hitched his belt. "If you ask me, I'd get out while the getting is good."

WELL IF THE police weren't going to do their job, Garrett figured grimly that he'd do it for them. He took photographs of the desecration, including a close-up of the turd that had him barely holding down the pizza he'd eaten while out shopping. He scooped the foul thing up as best he could with an old copy of the *Boston Beacon*, held it out at arm's length as he rushed to the bathroom, flushed the turd down the toilet, flushed another two times, then triple-bagged the soiled paper and set it outside on the porch.

He'd find out who had done this and make them pay. He wasn't a violent man, and he didn't know what he'd do, or even how he'd catch whoever had done this, but he'd make them pay.

He would make... them... pay.

But who was he kidding? If the police weren't even remotely interested, he and his family had no chance to get justice. They were powerless against an entire neighborhood that hated them.

All because of the color of their skin.

Garrett tried to think of a plan as he stripped down the beds, trying to ignore the stench of the urine, then loaded the washer with the stained sheets and covers and set out to scrub down the mattresses, wondering if he should just haul them off to the dump and buy new ones.

How could he find out who had done this? He had only dumb ideas. But he supposed dumb ideas were better than none at all.

As Bea bundled the girls up to go with her to her mother's apartment where the three of them would stay the night crammed in like sardines, she let Garrett know in no uncertain terms that she wasn't happy about leaving him behind, especially based on the first stage of the plan still formulating in his mind. His *damned-fool plan,* in her exact words. Before he tried anything else, he'd see if whoever had done this would come back for a repeat performance after the Harrison's only car left the driveway. Maybe even bring a few more friends for the fun.

"That's your plan?" she had said, incredulous. "What kind of a trap is that? A trap for them or for you?"

"I know it probably won't work," Garrett said. "It's just the first step—"

"I'm afraid of what happens if it *does* work. You think being here alone is a good idea? What if they do show up? You got no gun. It'll just be you and that knife against how many? Half a dozen of them? A dozen? Maybe with guns." She glared at him with steel in her eyes. "Maybe a rope."

That last one was a hit below the belt. It sent an icicle pick up and down Garrett's spine. Even if this was Massachusetts, not Mississippi.

But Bea couldn't argue with the logic that the girls had to be taken out of here—out of this dream home turned nightmare—while Garrett continued the clean-up effort. And the sooner the better.

So she tearfully hugged him, told him it was better to be safe than sorry. He'd be the better man, the smarter man, if he ran out the back door and fled intruders he couldn't hope to fight off rather than stay and get beaten to within an inch of his life. Or worse.

Garrett had nodded his agreement. Even though he knew there was no way he was going out that back door.

Not that it would ever come to that. He was sure that whoever had done this would never make a return visit. They'd taken their shot. They'd made their point. What more was there to gain by a repeat performance?

Garrett had learned over the years, however, to never

overestimate the intelligence of a bigot. Or underestimate the bigot's hatred and need to consume even more of his victim's soul.

If the fool, or fools, wandered into the trap of a presumably empty house, and tripped over the cord Garrett had stretched out near the front door that would send an entire row of books toppling to the ground, then he'd at least find out the identity of his enemy. If not, he would have at least been working the whole time on cleaning up this mess—nothing lost on that front—and if the enemy wouldn't come to him, then he'd just have to track down the enemy.

AS IT TURNED OUT, he was going to have to track down the enemy. All of them.

Garrett was no detective, but he was pretty sure there were three of them, maybe more. No way one person could have held all that urine to piss on all three beds. Not even a camel could hold that much.

So it had been three men, Garrett figured, or teenage boys. Or some combination of the two. Three or more. Most likely from right on this street.

The place he'd start looking would be with the ring-leaders of the effort to outbid him for the house and keep the neighborhood white. That would be Jerry O'Leary, three houses down, Tommy Callahan, five houses in the other direction, and Ryan O'Donnell, across the street. Those three plus the teenaged kid who'd given Garrett the finger-across-the-throat gesture. Probably had a name like Shamus O'Reilly. The Irish Catholics ran thick in these parts.

For this task, Garrett pulled on his navy blue winter jacket, grabbed something off the top shelf of his bedroom closet, checked it out, and tucked it inside the jacket. He shoved his bare hands into the jacket pockets, and walked out the door. He crossed the street to the O'Donnell house, a Cape Cod with a steep, snowless roof, gray wood siding and black shutters around white-framed windows.

Garrett rang the doorbell. It chimed loudly, and he swore he heard the padding of feet on the other side of the door, but no one answered.

He rang again.

And then a third time before he turned and left.

The kid with the throat-slicing gesture came next. Garrett could see from the mailbox, a custom wooden one cut into the shape of a dog's head and painted light brown, that the last name was Spinelli. For the briefest instant, Garrett wondered what an Italian family like Spinelli was doing in this Irish Catholic neighborhood, then realized that he was the last person who should be asking that question.

Garrett walked along the red brick walkway to the porch of the two-story, clapboard-sided house and rang the doorbell. Again, he heard a loud chime along with the rustling of feet on the other side, but this time it was accompanied by a loud barking of what sounded like a pretty big dog. The barking echoed loudly in what Garrett thought must be a cavernous foyer.

He waited. He glanced over at the basketball hoop

towering over the driveway. A slight wind blew cold air, a few scant degrees above freezing, over Garrett's face and exposed hands.

"Go away!" called out a female voice from inside.

Garrett supposed he should have expected this. "I just have a couple questions."

"I ain't opening the door to the likes of you!" More barking. "I'm not stupid."

"Then please just stand there and answer a couple questions," Garrett said, hating the pleading sound in his voice. "I just want to ask about what happened at my house yesterday."

"What happened? I saw the cops come, but I don't know nothing else."

Garrett wondered if she was lying. He didn't think so, but he wasn't sure.

"Somebody who really hates me and my family broke in and did some pretty awful things."

"So why are you asking me?"

"You have a son who's about eighteen or so? Black hair? Thin? Very thin?"

The woman paused before responding warily, "What if I do?"

"He saw me the other day and drew his finger across his throat," Garrett said.

Silence.

"Like he was cutting my throat."

"Yeah, I got it." She swore, setting off a new round of barking.

"You can see why he made the list of someone who hates my family."

"There ain't a soul on this street and most everyone on all the surrounding streets who ain't on that list of yours," the woman said. "Or at least who shouldn't be on it."

"Well, then I might have to talk to every soul on this street and all the others until I find out who did it."

"What did they do?" the woman asked with what seemed like an almost erotic interest.

But Garrett wasn't about to give her the satisfaction. "Good day, " he said, turned. and left.

GARRETT HIT pay dirt at the Callahan house, a tan ranch with white shutters and a two-car garage. Much like his own, except the garage.

And except for the spray-painted graffiti of pure venom. And the lingering smell of urine in the bedrooms. And Garrett suspected no one had taken a shit beneath the Christmas tree in this house.

So there were differences.

Garrett stabbed the doorbell. Inside it chimed and a young voice hollered, "I got it."

The door opened, and a little boy no more than five or six appeared, still in his red-and-black footie pajamas. His light brown hair shot in every direction. Behind him was a tan sofa and coffee table that faced a TV along the front wall. Off to the side stood a ten-foot-tall, brightly decorated Christmas tree.

Still erect. Presumably with no fecal matter beneath it.

Garrett smiled. "Hello, could I please speak to your mother or father?"

The kid turned his back and yelled, "Ma! It's the jig!"

The word pierced Garrett. Its casual use, as if that was simply his name.

The jig.

And from a kid so little. It was already so ingrained as to be second nature. Garrett could only imagine what the kid would be like in ten years.

A red-haired woman with pink curlers in her hair emerged from around the corner. Her eyes widened. She pointed at Garrett.

"Shut the door, Devin! Shut the door!"

Garrett knew full well what the woman was commanding her son to do but applying a large dose of deliberate misunderstanding, he stepped inside the door and slammed it shut.

"There it is!" Garrett said triumphantly, as if a difficult, important task had been accomplished. He smiled. "Sorry to have let the cold air inside."

The house smelled the way a house was supposed to smell this time of year. The pine scent of the Christmas tree mixed in with what had to be chocolate chip cookies baking in the oven.

"Get out!" the woman screamed. "Get out!" she repeated, this time adding the epithet that had been spray-painted all over Garrett's house.

Garrett thought he just might have found his family's tormentor. Or to be more accurate, the wife and mother of the tormentors. So he gambled. Knowing he was a dead man if anyone showed up with a gun as he stood there, he asked the sixty-four-thousand-dollar question.

"Why did your family do those unspeakable things to my house?"

The woman froze.

The little kid pointed at Garrett. "I went pee pee on your bed!" the kid said, laughing. "I went pee pee on your bed!" Garrett's jaw dropped. His heart sank as the little boy laughed harder and harder. "My daddy told me to. So I went pee pee on your bed."

Garrett stared at the woman. *The little boy?* Garrett had assumed it was the father and a couple friends or older brothers. But a five-year old child?

Mrs. Callahan thrust her jaw out defiantly. "You got what you deserved!" she said. "We don't regret a thing! You don't belong here and the sooner you leave the better for all of us."

"You and your husband brought your five-year-old son to help you?" Garrett asked, the pitch rising in his voice.

Mrs. Callahan smiled smugly. "The Bible says, 'Train up a child in the way he should go: and when he is old, he will not depart from it.' Devin was old enough to learn how we protect our own. How we protect him."

Garrett shook his head in disbelief. "Which one of you took the shit beneath the tree?"

The woman laughed uproariously . "*I did!* While Tommy and the boys were upstairs going number one, I was down here going number two. Why should the men have all the fun?" As she laughed harder and harder, her son joined in.

"Let me get this right," Garrett said. "You're Shannon Callahan, and you think it's *funny* that you defecated at the base of my family's Christmas tree?"

"Proud of it!" she said, and exploded into more laughter.

Garrett unzippered his navy blue jacket and pointed inside to the chrome-and-black, five-by-eight-inch Philips portable cassette recorder that was propped against his belt. Its red record light was lit, and the sprockets of the tape were smoothly turning. Its finger-thick microphone poked out from the bottom of his jacket.

"Would you like to hear yourself admitting your guilt of a federal crime?" Garrett asked. "The Civil Rights Act, passed in the days following the assassination of Dr. Martin Luther King earlier this year, prohibits what you have done."

The Callahan woman stared at Garrett. Her nostrils flared. "My husband is a personal friend of the chief of police in this town. During the summer, they play golf together two or three times a week. The chief will laugh in your face."

"It's a federal crime," Garrett said. Bluffing, he said, "I could go to the FBI."

Shannon Callahan called his bluff. "You think the FBI cares that I took a shit in your front room? J. Edgar Hoover hates you people almost as much as we do!"

Garrett gathered his thoughts. The woman was right there. She and her family were very much long shots to ever get charged with anything.

But there was always shame.

"If it comes down to it," Garrett said, "there's a very

popular columnist for the *Boston Beacon* who I am sure would love to tell his readers about you taking your five-year-old child to piss on a neighbor's bed. And I'm sure those readers would love to hear about you 'getting in on the fun' by taking a shit on the rug next to my family's Christmas tree.

"You don't get any better symbolism than that," Garrett continued. "Although I suspect he'll have to replace the phrase 'taking a shit' with 'defecate.' That way your son's kindergarten or first-grade class can read the column, too."

GARRETT DIDN'T BOTHER with either the local police or the FBI. He knew that Shannon Callahan was right about one thing. Both of those avenues were lost causes. Instead, he got Bea to race back to the house, and together they sped to the downtown *Boston Beacon* offices where they met with the paper's top columnist. They played the recording for him and handed him the not-yet-developed film from Garrett's camera.

Then not a damned thing happened.

Garrett had naively imagined a three-part series in the *Beacon* about the blatant housing discrimination from the urban streets on out to suburbs like this one. It would be titled "No better than Mississippi" with the subtitle "Outrage in the suburbs." The series would shame the Callahans and all the families like them, from the parents on down to five-year-olds following in the sins of their fathers and mothers. And perhaps the series would even force those sworn to uphold and enforce laws like the Civil Rights Act to actually do their damned jobs.

There would be justice. Or so Garrett dreamed.

But there was no three-part series. No three paragraphs. Not even three damned words.

Garrett called the *Beacon*, but the columnist wouldn't give him the time of day. "I'm sorry, but there's nothing I can do about it."

And so on Christmas morning, Garrett felt the bitterest of tastes in his mouth as he watched Marie and Janice sitting on the floor beside the tree, opening their presents. He and Bea had washed and scrubbed what had been defiled, and rewrapped and repurchased what had been torn apart and ruined.

But it wasn't the same. It would never be the same.

Garrett wasn't sure if the image of that turd underneath the tree would ever leave his mind. He would forever smell piss, and not the Lysol that had cleaned it, in the beds upstairs. He suspected he was not alone.

When the presents were all opened, it was time to say what had to be said. Bea had wondered if they couldn't wait just a bit longer and let the girls enjoy the holidays. But the haunted looks in both girls' eyes and their hollow laughter made a lie out of that hope.

"Girls, we have something to ask you," Garrett said. He and Bea sat beside each other on the sofa. The girls sat cross-legged, still in their pajamas, on the floor.

"We can sell the house and move out," Garrett said.

Shocked, the girls looked at Garrett, then Bea, then Garrett.

"Your mother and I don't want to move," he said, "but

there's no forgetting what happened. And we can't promise there won't be more trouble. We probably haven't seen the last of it. So if you want us to leave, we want you to say so."

Marie stared at the floor. Tears streamed down Janice's face as she looked down, too.

"Come up here, you two," Bea finally said, and slid away from Garrett and patted the seat between them. Silently, but for Janice's sobs, the girls moved to the sofa, sat down, and they all hugged. All but Garrett cried, and inside, his heart broke, too.

Again.

"Daddy, what do you think we should do?" Janice asked, as Bea wiped away her tears.

Garrett looked to Marie, who said nothing.

"I don't want to tell you how to think, but..." He took a deep breath. "Rosa Parks didn't run when she was told to move to the back of the bus. James Meredith didn't run when whites rioted because he was going to become the first black man to enter the University of Mississippi. Vivian Malone didn't run when George Wallace tried to block her from entering the University of Alabama.

"If we run, the forces of evil in this neighborhood win. And then it will be even more difficult for the next black family like us to survive where we failed. So your mother and I don't want to run. We don't want to leave.

"But Dr. Martin Luther King also didn't run. And he paid the ultimate price. We might have to pay the ultimate price."

The words cut Garrett like a knife, but there was no sugarcoating the truth.

Silence fell over them all. There were no good answers.

After a time, Bea softly began to sing "We Shall Overcome." The girls joined in first, and then Garrett.

In unison, they sang for a long time, then cried for even longer.

SQUIRREL AND WORM

INTRODUCTION TO SQUIRREL
AND WORM

As a participant in a workshop on combining romance and spy fiction, I was assigned several novels to read along with my choice of three nonfiction books, one of which was *Madame Fourcade's Secret War: The Daring Young Women Who Led France's Largest Spy Network Against Hitler.*

I don't recall precisely why I chose that title over the others. Probably it was nothing more earth-shatteringly brilliant than, "I guess this one looks good." Followed by starting to read it and being totally incapable of putting the book down.

Holy smokes, did I get lucky! The book didn't just bowl me over. It knocked me ass over teakettle.

I couldn't wait to write about my own fictional spies comparable to those in real life who risked, and often gave, their lives in the fight against Hitler. I pounced on the opportunity. The result was the initial version of "Squirrel and Worm."

I liked it. A lot.

Then along came my friend M.L. ("Matt") Buchman who was starting a new quarterly magazine called *Thrill Ride* dedicated exclusively to thriller short stories. Even better, one issue's theme was *Honor*. I considered "Squirrel and Worm" a bullseye for that one and submitted it with high hopes.

Matt considered it... a maybe.

The problem was that too much of the story lacked a thriller's tension. What was tense was really, really, really tense. But much of the rest? Not enough. Not enough for a thriller.

Matt made some suggestions and I took a shot and sent it back, but in truth, it was only a half-hearted shot. I had my vision for the story. And I'm instinctively stubborn almost to the point of absurdity. I simply wasn't willing to compromise. I've written in previous of these introductions how important it is to follow your own vision for a story. Compromise can be death to a writer's soul. Plus that Hendrickson stubborn thing.

It was far too late to write another story and submit it as a replacement, so I resigned myself to going 1-for-2 with my efforts to get into *Thrill Ride*'s inaugural year. (Matt had already accepted "Too Many Idiots, Too Few Boats" for *Thrill Ride: Betrayal*. Look for it in my upcoming collection *Crime, Up Close and Personal*, scheduled to release two months after this volume.) Batting .500 isn't the worst thing in the world even when you're perpetually shooting for 1.000.

Matt, however—gotta love the guy—didn't give up. He approached—attacked?—from another angle, and suddenly the light went off beside my thick skull. I didn't have to compromise my vision for the story. Not at all. Matt was showing me how to *improve* it.

Emails flew back and forth at a furious rate. Revisions. Suggestions. Tweaks. More revisions, suggestions, and tweaks.

In the end, thanks to Matt's persistence and thriller expertise, I had a story I had once liked *a lot* but now *loved*. So much better than the original.

I *adore* this story. It's one of those that just makes me feel warm and good all over. Perhaps because it's really good. Or perhaps simply because in the end it took all that extra effort to push it across the finish line, so the result feels all the more satisfying.

It's probably impossible for you to love this story as much as I do.

But please, give it a try.

SQUIRREL AND WORM

March, 1944

Springtime in Paris had always been magical for Monique Bardet and for so many reasons. Cherry blossoms at the Notre Dame Cathedral. The Luxembourg gardens in full bloom. Outdoor cafés filled with happy couples, the smells of freshly brewed coffee and *croissants* wafting from their canopied tables. Walking along the Seine, crisp gusts of air lifting her flowing blonde hair off her slender shoulders as if each strand was but a feather.

But there was nothing magical about springtime in Paris now. Nor had there been for the last four years since German troops marched into the city after the traitor Philippe Pétain surrendered the country under the pretext of an armistice and its illusion of country still partially free.

Now, German soldiers and officials sat at the café tables. German plays had corrupted the *Théâtre des Champs-Élysées,* and the Berlin Philharmonic had taken its seats at the *Opéra Garnier* while the red Nazi flags with their loathsome swastikas, black against a circle of white, flew outside. Framed against the *Arc de Triomphe*, German tanks and goose-stepping soldiers had paraded down the *Champs-Élysées*.

Arc de Triomphe? More like *Arc de Défaite*.

Not if Monique could help it. Twenty-one years old, the youngest of three children of well-to-do parents, she'd watched her two older brothers, Étienne and Lucien, thought to be beyond the reach of the Third Reich since the family was wealthy and not Jewish, conscripted into the German war effort by the *service du travail obligatoire*. They'd been deported to Nazi Germany to work as forced labor in the factories.

And so now she found herself bustling along the *Boulevard Saint-Germain*, the hundred-page-thick package of *trés dangereux* documents taped to her thin, flat stomach, hidden beneath her light yellow dress and its dozen buttons down the front. Though the spring day was *parfait* with the sun poking through the cottony clouds and a light breeze blowing in her face, sweat still trickled down her forehead, stinging her eyes and dampening the brow of her fashionable light yellow hat.

Slow down, Monique told herself, wiping dry her brow. *Blend in.*

She forced herself to move no faster than a casual stroll, despite the urgency. *Especially* because of the urgency. *Trés dangereux*. The documents burned like hot flames against her stomach.

She saw danger everywhere. Every man seated in the café she passed on the right was not merely ogling her as men had done for so many years; he was a Gestapo agent. Every woman in the long line at the *pâtisserie* glancing at her while waiting for the meager rationed bread and flour was not just envying her youth and good looks; no, those women were collaborators, eager to report her to the Gestapo for a few francs or an extra ration of bread or simply to shift the crosshairs from themselves to someone, anyone else.

Monique had been acting as a courier for Alliance, a secret intelligence arm of *la résistance*, for over a year now. But though she excelled at it, especially using her beauty and apparent light, carefree attitude to escape danger, she always knew that her first capture would likely be her last. Her heart thundered with every mission even as her responsibilities grew in the form of documents increasingly more vital to the cause. And increasingly more dangerous if she were caught.

This was the first time the words *"trés dangereux"* had been whispered to her when given the documents. As if by comparison all their predecessors had been mere child's play.

And so Monique's heart hammered and her mouth grew dry as she saw danger everywhere, knowing she probably was right. No amount of experience, even with her record of over a year without a single arrest, could make this *juste un autre jour*, just another day.

She suddenly felt the shock of a large, meaty hand groping her bottom. Monique yelped and whirled on a stocky, fair-skinned, blond-haired, blue-eyed man about her age. Classic Aryan features. Smiling broadly.

He winked. *"Danke."*

Then he brushed past her with a laugh and another grope. "*Ich nehme, was ich will.*" I'll take what I want.

Monique's face flushed with anger. It wasn't the first time she'd been groped, and it certainly wouldn't be the last, though that made it no less degrading. Until the occupation, it had been her fellow countrymen who had taken liberties with their hands, pinching and squeezing and caressing where their hands did not belong. She would never get used to it, but it had stopped surprising her.

Coming from a German these days, however, made it worse. In all matters, the Germans knew they could take what they wanted and laugh about it in the process. Would the degradations never end? Being glad he hadn't taken more made her feel no better.

Monique took a deep breath and gathered herself. Deliver the package. *Trés dangereux.* She licked her dry lips, turned left, walked two blocks, turned right and headed for the grime-stained, four-story office building at number 237. She took the stairs to the fourth floor, walked down the hallway to the specified room on the right and gave three sharp knocks.

"Who goes there?" came the muffled command from inside the room.

Monique replied with the designated code words. The voice inside replied in kind.

"*Vive la France!*" she said, as specified.

The door opened and she stepped into a small, square office not even five meters wide with a single battered desk and chair facing out and a rectangular table along the right wall.

"Are you Worm?" Monique asked.

"Are you Squirrel?" the man—dressed in a sharp brown suit, white shirt, and navy blue tie—replied.

With the official sequence complete to verify that they were each the agents the other expected, Monique let out a sigh of relief. Or at least half a sigh of relief. The other half could come after she turned over the package of documents taped to her stomach and got back out onto the street and *très dangereux* would be a thing of the past. Her heart could stop jackhammering, sweat would not cling to her clothes as if she were a grimy fieldhand on a midsummer day, and she could at least dream of smelling like a lady.

Then she looked again at the man known as Worm— *really* looked at him—and caught her breath all over again. Worm could not be more poorly named. About her age, he was staggeringly handsome with wavy brown hair, a bright, charming smile, and pale gray eyes that seemed to be full of mirth despite the gravity of their circumstance.

Monique wasn't a believer in love at first sight. Past romantic debacles had left her wondering if love existed at all. But if she did still believe in it magically happening at first sight, this man could have qualified as Exhibit A. He could not be any more dashing. Especially those pale gray eyes that somehow seemed to smile. She was no foolish schoolgirl, swooning over the first handsome man she met while forgetting the life-and-death stakes of what they were doing, but she also was not blind. This man could make the American movie actor Clark Gable jealous.

"Worm?" Monique asked again, though not really asking it as a question. "How could anyone have given you that name?"

"I lost a bet," he said, bemused.

And if her eyes didn't deceive her, he appeared as taken with her, at least on first glance, as she was with him.

"Let's take care of business," she said. The papers taped to her stomach were all but burning against her skin. She moved to the left side of the desk. "Turn around."

The man known only as Worm frowned for a brief second, then nodded and turned his back to her. She turned her back as well and began unbuttoning the front of her dress.

Worm chuckled. "My kingdom for two mirrors."

Ignoring him, Monique pulled free the package of documents from their strapping to her stomach and set the package on the desk. She ripped the loose strapping free from her skin and hurriedly buttoned up her dress. Picking up the package, she turned and held it out to Worm.

His back was still to her.

"*Pardonnez-moi,*" he said. "My comment was meant to lighten our dark situation, but was not one made by a gentleman. And so I am sorry. Your beauty turned my mind and my manners to *bouillie.*"

Monique nodded. Worm's apology seemed sincere and he had an undeniable charm to go with his staggering good looks. But this was no time for small talk or flirtation.

"Perhaps we will meet again," Monique said, and turned to leave.

"Forgive me for noticing, but the buttons on your lovely dress are no longer properly aligned."

Monique looked down and flushed. In her rush to re-button her dress as quickly as possible and escape this *trés dangereux* place, she'd put the top button in the second hole, the second button in the third, and all the way down. *Mon Dieu!* Worm no doubt was hoping she would re-button herself immediately—*my kingdom for two mirrors*—but she would not take the time. As soon as she was out of this building, she would find an appropriate place to fix her mistake.

"Thank you, but I must leave immediately," Monique said, and stepped toward the door.

"Tomorrow night?" Worm asked and named a local bar.

Before she even had a moment to consider the offer, the door thundered with a pounding from outside.

Eyes wide, Monique whirled to face Worm. He appeared every bit as shocked as she was.

Before either of them even had a chance to respond, the door splintered open with a crash.

"Gestapo! Don't move!" yelled the first of six Gestapo agents who poured into the room, Walther pistols drawn. Trailing them was the stocky, blond-haired, blue-eyed Nazi pig who had groped Monique on the street.

He seemed surprised to see her. A leering grin formed on his face as he eyed her misbuttoned dress up and down.

"What do we have here?" he asked. "Seize the man and the package!"

Monique turned and stared at Worm, who appeared to be forlorn as he handed the package over. But was that just an act? Was he a secret German agent, betraying her and all of the Alliance network? Had his flirtatious comments been meant solely to delay her until his collaborators arrived?

"*Traitor*!" she screamed at him.

Worm recoiled. "*Me?* Never!"

"Take the man away!" the Nazi pig commanded. "Schmidt, keep your weapon trained on the *fräulein*. She appears to have undressed since we last met just minutes ago. I will question her myself."

WORM, whose real name was Henri Leclerc, came to. Following an agonizing interrogation and beating, he was now lying on the hard wooden floor of a barren room no more than three meters wide and deep. It stank of sweat, vomit, and piss. Most likely, his own. His suit coat and tie were gone. His white shirt and brown trousers clung to his body, wrinkled and bloodied. Slivers of pain shot through his eyeballs. He licked his cracked lips and tasted blood. Every muscle in his body ached with deep, fresh bruises.

Henri was surprised he was still alive. Probably not for long. Only night leaked in through the padlocked window. *La résistance* had taught the Nazis that they did not own the night. They would wait for dawn to either publicly execute him, or drag him to the airfield for questioning in Berlin.

From the faint sounds below, it sounded as if Paris was going to sleep for the night. Few vendors hawked their wares at such an hour and horse's hooves clopping on streets long since rendered empty of automobiles shuffled slowly. Henri surmised that he was on an upper floor somewhere, perhaps the hotel at *84 Avenue Foch* commandeered by the Gestapo for its Paris headquarters and where it was rumored to house prisoners it considered especially important on the top floor.

Important. *Wonderful.*

He forced himself to move, to inspect his prison. A boarded up exit, presumably to a balcony, and a padlocked window on the wall opposite the stout door. Henri longed to look outside and confirm or deny his wild guess, but for now, he could no more get to his feet than he could jump to the moon.

Un moment, he told himself. *Un moment.*

The previous day's memories flooded over him like acid on bare skin. It had begun so wonderfully. He had not believed his eyes when the agent known as Squirrel walked in the door to the Alliance office. Since when was the most beautiful woman in the world allowed to be a courier? And not just any courier. The one chosen to deliver to him some of the most important secrets for *la résistance*.

And when he'd suggested that they meet again at his favorite bar, he'd seen in her lovely green eyes that despite his unfortunate quip about the mirrors so he could see her unbuttoned dress—surely a forgivable slip of the tongue for any man with a pulse—he had a chance. She'd appeared to be close to agreeing to see him again.

But that dream blew up when the Gestapo thugs burst through the splintered office door. And Henri's heart had sank—been *crushed*—when the lead Gestapo agent in plain clothes said the most heartbreaking words Henri had heard in his life.

"The *fräulein* appears to have undressed since we last met just minutes ago," the lead Gestapo agent had said with a knowing smile.

Since we last met just minutes ago.

Of course, Agent Squirrel had been too good to be true. Supposedly a highly respected Alliance courier—if not *the* best of them all based on the codes and secrets entrusted to her in that package—Squirrel had also been jaw-dropping gorgeous.

Too good to be true.

A double agent. Of course. A whore to the Gestapo.

No doubt arranging his own betrayal. Perhaps while sleeping with the enemy. Then had had the nerve to scream in his face, "*Traitor!*"

Mirrors were called for after all. At least one, that is, so Double Agent Squirrel could see her admittedly beautiful, but ultimately duplicitous and vilely traitorous face.

See the image of the true traitor. Whose betrayal had caused the loss of the critical documents—the Gestapo had burst in so fast he'd had no time to burn or eat even a single page—and led to his own capture, and an endless evening spent in a dank, dark interrogation room.

Was this even the same night? Or had his interrogation taken two or three? He'd passed out too many times to be sure. Perhaps, if it was the same night—and he could escape the most secure Gestapo prison in all Paris—he could sound the alarm in time that the vital documents were in Gestapo hands. By midday tomorrow, all would be lost. It could set the Alliance back years, if not permanently.

"The *fraulein* has told us everything about your intelligence operation, as have a hundred other of your captured spies," his dark-haired, black-eyed, cold-hearted inquisitor said over and over between beatings. "We know everything. Tell us what we already know. It will hurt nothing and save your life. Otherwise, we will torture you and send you to one of the camps."

But Henri had divulged nothing and eventually passed out from the beating. And now, here he was in this tiny, barren room.

Waiting to die.

He closed his eyes and listened again to the sounds in the street below. This had to be the fourth or fifth floor, he figured. Too high to jump out of the far-too-small window and survive.

Slowly, he attempted to get on all fours. The room swayed. His gut roiled. Henri clenched his eyes shut and gritted his teeth.

He crawled to the nearest wall. Leaning against it for support, he set one foot flat on the floor and pushed up as best he could. His leg wobbled but with the wall's aid, he staggered to his feet.

The room spun even more fiercely now.

Henri sucked in gasps of air. Pain screamed inside his head. He tasted blood.

But he was alive.

He lurched toward the window, made it halfway, then crashed to the floor. He lay on the hard, wooden surface and tried to hold back the vomit.

Suddenly, he was aware of a soft tapping coming from low on the right wall. At first, Henri wanted to scream for it to stop. Every tap shot more slivers of pain through his eyeballs and skull.

But belatedly, he realized the taps came in long and short sequences.

Morse code.

Henri choked back his excitement and crawled to the wall. The message, initially half complete, repeated itself over and over.

... YOU OKAY?

ARE YOU OKAY?

ARE YOU...

Henri tapped back and the other room instantly went silent.

FINE, he tapped. BETRAYED. CAPTURED. BEATEN. DID NOT TALK. FINE NOW.

Until they ship me to Berlin tomorrow.

GOOD, came the response. SOUNDED IN A BAD WAY.

That was one way of putting it. Locked up in Gestapo headquarters, it couldn't be much worse.

?84 AVENUE FOCH, TOP FLOOR ABOVE GESTAPO HQ? Henri responded. USED FOR IMPOR-TANT PRISONERS.

FIFTH FLOOR, came the response. BUT 142 FOCH. SAW ADDRESS WHEN BROUGHT HERE. WHO ARE YOU?

Henri took a long time to respond. He never divulged information except to those who absolutely needed to know. He even hesitated with a superior he was unfamiliar with. He'd said nothing last night, not even useless trivialities. And it was possible the person on the other side of the wall was a Gestapo agent, posing as a fellow captured prisoner.

But a Gestapo agent likely would not have freely given information about their location and Henri would only reply now with his code name.

I AM...

No, he would not trust that much.

A PATRIOT. YOU?

MONIQUE HAD FEARED the worst when the groping Nazi bastard named *Müller* sent the others away, save for the man he called Schmidt to keep his Walther pointed at her. *Müller* ordered her to remove all her clothes—"to be certain you are not hiding other secrets," he had said in an outrageous explanation—and then eyed her lasciviously.

Standing there, her hands clasped behind her back as ordered so she could not cover herself, humiliated and violated by the man's cold eyes, she readied herself for the meaty hands that had groped her down on the avenue. His loathsome touch would be upon her bare flesh this time. And then, the unthinkable.

Instead, only his eyes probed her naked body. He questioned her for hour after hour in that thoroughly subjugated, humiliated state, smoke from his cigarette filling the air. Through it all, her sole solace was imagining that her fingernails were the claws of a lioness with which she would shred Worm's pretty face.

Then *Müller* threatened worse.

"It would be a shame," *Müller* said, "for such a beautiful body to be scarred by burns from this cigarette."

Monique suppressed a shudder and told him nothing.

"Burns on your beautiful breasts. Burns on the most sensitive parts of your body," he said. "Or perhaps on that lovely, unblemished face."

She told him nothing.

"Or Schmidt could hold you down for my pleasure and when I have had my fill of your luscious body, Schmidt could take a turn."

She told him nothing, but this time could not suppress the shudder. The Nazi pig laughed at her discomfort, even more so as her entire body trembled and tears streamed down her face no matter how she tried to stop them.

In her mind, Monique began to recite the only words she could think of to distance herself from this horror. *Hail Mary, full of grace, the Lord is with thee. Blessed art thou amongst women...*

Perhaps the Blessed Virgin interceded on her behalf, Monique thought later, so that the Nazi pig never touched her. Or perhaps he had found that the violation of his eyes was sufficient to give him the desired satisfaction of total subjugation. Or perhaps, Monique shuddered uncontrollably at this thought, the pig was holding in reserve the acting out of his threats for the days to come.

Whatever the case, he did not touch her. *Praise be to the Blessed Virgin.*

Finally, *Müller* had ordered Monique to get dressed and summoned additional guards to bring her to the tiny, barren room on the fifth floor of the old hotel building at *142 Avenue Foch.* Exhausted physically and even more so emotionally and spiritually, she collapsed on the hard, wooden floor, barely lit by thin streams of sunlight slipping in through the padlocked window.

She must have slept, for she awoke to darkness as a body crashed into the next room. She blinked and tried to remember where she was. It hit her fast enough. She recoiled as if struck.

A prisoner of the Gestapo. On *Avenue Foch.* Her days most certainly numbered.

Monique pulled herself up from the floor, her muscles cramped and aching. She'd inspected the window upon her arrival. There was little point of doing it again in the darkness when only moonlight and perhaps a few pale streetlights kept her from total darkness, but she was drawn to it anyway.

The thin, vertically rectangular window looked out onto the street, five stories below. Hours earlier, before darkness fell, two men had ridden bicycles past, another sat in a horse-drawn cart, and a Citroen motored off to her left, its red Nazi flag flapping as it moved. Another hotel almost a twin of this one stood on other side of the street. The room to her left enjoyed a metal-railed balcony, presumably with its access from inside securely boarded up, but her corner room had none, only a crumbling brick ledge no wider than her foot was long.

The window itself consisted of thick metal molding on all sides and down the middle, splitting it into two halves. The molding encased two thin vertical strips of glass, breakable to be sure and a meter in height but only about a quarter of a meter wide. Even if every last shard were removed, Monique doubted she could slide her thin frame through one of two the openings, especially while crouched to duck into its one-meter height. In its past incarnation as part of a hotel room, as opposed to an improvised prison cell, the two halves of the window swung wide open to both sides, but now, an imposing padlock held the two sides locked together.

Following the German occupation, Monique had mastered lock-picking to a modest degree and had woven hairpins into the hem of all her skirts. But even if she could crack this lock—a very big if—what good would that do? The window opened only to the crumbling ledge below. If she somehow got to the neighboring balcony without plummeting to her death, what could she do then? If this room included a bed, she could use sheets to lower herself down, but the room included nothing. Even her dress would be of no use should she take it off. It was made of such thin material that it would never support even her meager weight.

The situation had looked hopeless in daylight and felt even worse now in the near total darkness of the room.

Which she supposed was the point. Prisons, even improvised ones like this, weren't supposed to be escapable. The best she could hope for, if she could pick the lock, would be a swift plummet to her death if she threw herself out of the window to avoid the torture that surely loomed.

A suicide that would doom her immortal soul to the pits of Hell.

At times like this, when she needed her Catholic faith the most, it seemed to fail her. Well, that was a bleak thought for another time. She'd say a hundred Hail Marys tonight in a show of contrition, but right now, she needed to figure a way out.

She studied the padlock more closely in the near pitch black darkness, loathe to remove any hairpins from the hem of her dress until she was actually ready to use them. If caught with them, she would be subjected to a body search beyond what the Gestapo pig had put her through and then all of her clothing would follow.

Figure out a plan first. Then act.

From the room to her left, Monique heard a muffled, agonized groan. She cocked her head. She'd heard no guards in the hallway since her neighbor had been tossed into his room. The floor was presumably considered secure with perhaps only the stairways guarded.

The groan sounded again. A fellow prisoner? It had to be. It sounded like he—it was definitely a man from the sound of it—was in great pain. Monique moved to the wall, lay down on the hard floor, and pressed her ear to the wall.

More agonized groans.

She listened for the sound of any guards with their unmistakable heavy boots.

Nothing.

It could be a trap, of course. A Gestapo agent waiting for her to divulge secrets. Not a comrade at all. But Monique doubted it. Besides, there were some chances you just had to take.

In Morse code, she tapped the most benign message possible, one that would cause her no significant trouble even if it was a Gestapo agent in that room. Not so loud that it would echo down the hallway, but loud enough to still be heard in the room next door.

ARE YOU OKAY?

No response.

ARE YOU OKAY? she repeated.

The only response was the man's groans.

ARE YOU OKAY?

She repeated the message over and over. It seemed pointless, but what else was there for her to do?

Finally, the sound of staggering footsteps within the room and then of a body collapsing to the floor added to those of the groans.

ARE YOU OKAY?

Finally, the man responded.

FINE, he tapped. BETRAYED. CAPTURED. BEATEN. DID NOT TALK. FINE

Despite the dire circumstances they both faced, Monique breathed a sigh of relief. After correcting his almost dead-on correct guess that they were at *84 Avenue Foch,* needing to change only the number, she asked who he was. She supposed it wasn't important. What was important would be his abilities and if somehow his and hers could combine to hit the longest of long shots and get them out of here.

He took what felt like forever to reply, making her wonder if she'd overstepped her bounds. If perhaps he thought her foolish enough to be asking for a real name and identity.

He finally did reply.

A PATRIOT.

Not a name, but somehow even better. Hope soared into her, revitalizing her beyond reason. Even if it was a lie, she would choose to die believing it.

For so long she had felt she did her duty as a courier. Now, *now*, she would do so much more. She'd have to do so much more to escape and survive. Kill every Gestapo in all of Paris herself if she had to.

But she wasn't alone, if the man in the next room could be believed, and she did believe him. So she sent back the same reply, hoping it would revitalize him as well.

A PATRIOT.

Henri blinked. He wasn't sure if it was a horror that he was not the only one trapped here or pure relief that here was someone who might understand.

CAN YOU DELIVER A WARNING? he tapped.

FROM HERE??

Henri could hear the derisive laugh behind the unfeeling Morse code.

WE MUST ESCAPE. PEOPLE I MUST WARN.

He held his breath. So much rested on the response.

TOGETHER?

ALL FOR ONE, he sent.

AND ONE FOR ALL, the prisoner next door replied.

There would also be another matter. For Henri alone. Finding the beautiful, green-eyed traitor might be as impossible as the escape plan he and the other prisoner began hatching. But Henri swore he would do it if it was the last thing he did.

He *would* find her and he *would* kill her.

THEY LAUNCHED their escape shortly after two in the morning. The Paris streets had fallen truly silent and almost totally dark. They dared not delay. Monique's greatest fear was that one of them would be dragged away for interrogation or worse before they could attempt their outrageous plan. She was surprised it hadn't happened already.

MAYBE, Monique had tapped, SOMEONE ELSE IS HIGHER ON THE TORTURE PRIORITY LIST, prompting more gallows-humor smiling on both sides of the wall. It had been but one of a multitude of messages flying back and forth, most of them tactical, but some humorous.

She wondered who her fellow patriot might be. By his

education, an elderly professor. By his sharp wit, a teen. And by his steadfast dedication, exactly what she needed.

They knew their plan was almost certain to fail. The odds against them seemed astronomical. A thousand and one things could go wrong. But they'd agreed to die trying rather than cede the task to the Gestapo.

And so, when both of their internal clocks suggested it was two o'clock and the coast was as clear as they could get, Monique removed the padlock to her window that she'd picked an hour earlier. It had taken only five minutes but felt like five hours. For long minutes she'd wondered if the lock was going to foil the escape before it even started. But then it sprang open with a satisfying pop. She'd repositioned it so it still appeared closed, tapped disguised news of her success to her companion, and waited.

It was the longest hour of her life. They conversed little.

Now, Monique grabbed the cold metal molding and swung wide open the window. She looked out onto the dark, moonlit, starry sky and wondered if this would be her last. All of the early risks were hers. Not by design, but necessity. She licked her dry lips and boosted herself up to straddle the base of the open window.

She was tempted to look all the way down through the near total darkness to the ground below. Five stories down. Five stories down to the cold, rock-hard, unyielding street below. But Monique knew that would be a mistake.

As it was, she'd have enough trouble *not* seeing five stories down when she stepped out onto the treacherous ledge. Barely as wide as her feet were long. A brick ledge that in the harsh sunlight of day had appeared to be crumbling already with age.

But what else could she do?

Monique remembered the last words tapped between her and her fellow prisoner before the final go-ahead.

IF I DIE, he had tapped, I HOPE IT CAN BE SAVING YOUR LIFE.

The words had taken her breath away. She had responded with tear-filled eyes, blurting out—as much as one could blurt anything out in Morse code—the emotions flooding her heart.

I FEEL THE SAME WAY.

And to launch the escape, they simultaneously tapped:

ALL FOR ONE, AND ONE FOR ALL.

Monique repeated the words silently as she lifted her other leg up inside the window—her light yellow dress rising immodestly but unavoidably to her hips—so she was no longer straddling the window frame but was facing out, both legs dangling down.

Down.

The scariest of words right now. So Monique substituted the words that gave her as much peace and courage as she could muster right now.

All for one, and one for all.

Slowly, carefully, painstakingly, she turned inside the window frame. And lowered herself until her bare feet touched the ledge, the tips of her toes up against the rough brick wall.

Still clinging to the window frame, her chest just

beneath her breasts tight to the cold metal, she tested the ledge, letting more and more of her weight shift from her arms to her feet until only her fingertips touched the inside of the frame.

This part of the ledge was solid, *seemed* solid, but reflexively she clung back to the window frame, holding on for dear life. Her heart jackhammered. Sweat poured off her forehead and stung her eyes despite the cool evening breeze.

She wiped her brow with the back of her right hand and blinked fast.

All for one, and one for all.

Again, Monique let her weight shift to her feet. Again, until nothing but her fingertips touched the cold metal window frame.

A bitter taste filled her mouth. She caught a whiff of her ripe odor.

If I make it to him, she thought wryly, he might refuse to escape with someone so foul. She shook her head at such foolishness. She might smell, but he'd been beaten. They'd be quite the pair, if she got to him.

Gestapo thugs.

Thinking the two words got her moving.

Facing straight ahead at the window, thinking only "face straight ahead," not even letting the negative thought of "don't look down" enter her mind, she held onto the right side of the window frame for balance with her right hand. Then crossed over her left hand to grip it.

Slowly, painfully slowly yet feeling it was all too fast, Monique turned 180 degrees until the middle of her back, instead of her lower chest, was flat against the window frame and the back of her heels, instead of her toes, were against the gritty, brick wall.

With a gulp of air, she began edging along the ledge, face straight ahead, the back of her head scraping against the rough brick surface, the palms of her hands and fingertips flat against the bricks.

Tiny step by tiny step. Testing what seemed like every centimeter for its ability to support her weight.

Step by tiny step.

Until the window frame was no longer within her reach.

Step by tiny step.

Into the no-man's land halfway to the balcony railing outside her neighbor's room, shrouded in a darkness broken only by the meager illumination of the moonlight, cloaked every few seconds by a passing cloud.

No turning back now.

All for one, and one for all. All for one, and one for all. All for one, and one for all.

Step by step.

The ledge began to crumble beneath her right foot.

Faster step by faster step.

Two meters away. More crumbling.

Faster still. Even worse crumbling.

Chunks of the ledge tumbled down to the street far below. Five stories down. *Down, down, down.*

Smashing into the street with a loud splat.

Don't look down! Don't look down!

All for one, and one for all. All for one, and one for all. All for one, and one for all.

One meter away. So close.

So close and yet so far.

Faster. So close. The balcony railing was almost within reach.

So very close.

But suddenly not even visible as cloud cover extinguished even the moonlight.

The ledge beneath her feet cracked loudly. She felt it giving way.

Monique turned sideways. Took one last step. And with just enough leverage, lunged through the bleak darkness for where she hoped the balcony railing still waited.

Snagged it. Got her left foot on the base of the railing. And then the right.

Lifted one leg over the railing. Then the other.

And toppled onto the balcony into a heap.

HENRI WAITED INSIDE HIS ROOM, powerless. What was once an exit to the balcony had been securely boarded up long ago. The only access was through the thin rectangular window, padlocked shut and far too small for him to get through without breaking the lock. He'd tried to break it by brute force without success, and with nothing in the barren room remotely helpful for him to pick it, he remained imprisoned, awaiting his fellow prisoner's arrival. As planned, he'd broken the window glass and torn his trousers and shirt into strips no wider than the length of his foot, then tied them together to form the longest makeshift rope he could manage.

Now, he could only wait, wearing nothing but his bloodied underwear, holding his breath as the vague shape of his savior edged through the darkness closer to him. Back flat against the brick wall. Step by agonizing step. Each one seeming to take hours.

And yet he'd wait all night if she made it and they got free. But would she make it? He'd only learned of her gender when she'd communicated that her dress was of flimsy cloth having no use in creating a rope. He'd spent the long hours picturing an Amazonian savior, with flowing dark red hair to her waist. Henri knew it was ridiculous, but it passed the time.

When the brick ledge crumbled beneath her foot, he lunged involuntarily toward the window, arm extended, even while knowing the opening was far less than the width he needed to get through. His bruised shoulder crashed against the metal framing, and he stifled an agonized cry.

Then he barely contained a shriek of euphoria when her dark shadow lunged for the railing, grasped hold of it, and held on. Got her footing. Lifted a leg over the railing. Then toppled onto it.

She made it! She didn't plummet to her death!

She lay on the balcony floor for what felt like forever. Henri wanted to call out, make sure she was all right, but he knew they had to remain as quiet as possible. That no alarm had been sounded due to the falling masonry was miracle enough and he didn't want to test its limits.

Finally, she got to her feet, shook her head as if to clear the cobwebs, and stepped to his window.

Cloud cover had rendered her no more than a silhouette in the darkness. He could only assume that her actions were following the plan. Fish two hairpins from the hem of her dress. Put one between her teeth. Reach inside the window through the opening created when he broke the glass. Grasp the padlock with her free hand—this much he could see, so close it was—and blindly try to perform her magic.

She slid the first hairpin inside the lock and bent it down. Then slid the other in atop the first and jiggled it.

And jiggled it some more. And kept jiggling.

No luck.

Despair rose within Henri as her manipulations, barely visible in the almost total darkness, failed. Time after time, she wiggled the top hairpin. Time after time, the lock held firm. She'd popped hers while facing it square on—not by reaching through a window while perched on a balcony, wondering how soon she be raked by a searchlight then gunfire.

Minutes that felt like hours passed.

Henri wanted to scream his frustration. She had somehow managed the torturous tightrope walk across the ledge. It felt abjectly unfair for her to navigate that only to fail to pop this lock.

"Let me try," Henri whispered after more minutes that felt like hours.

Ignoring him, she wiggled the top hairpin. Jiggled it. Yanked it in and out.

"You'll have to leave without me," Henri whispered, though he knew she couldn't make it alone.

She gestured angrily, dismissing the idea.

Then got back to work.

Manipulating the hairpin. Jiggling it up and down. In and out.

Until...

The padlock popped open!

She did it!

She backed away on the balcony, staggering uneasily. Looked to the heavens. Crossed herself.

Henri swung open the window and climbed out into the cold. He wore only his bloodstained and grime-covered underwear, the makeshift rope made of strips of his trousers and shirt in his hands. As the clouds parted to bathe them in moonlight, he turned to face her.

You!!!

Monique almost shrieked the word aloud. Her mind and soul most certainly screamed it. She stabbed an accusatory index finger at the filthy traitor. Only her instinctive terror of what awaited her if she were captured kept that one word and so many others somehow bottled up inside.

Traitor!

She felt murderous rage. But it was a helpless murderous rage. She was no match for him. Had no weapon. She backed away. Had to get away from him.

It had been a trap. She'd been a fool! Of course it had been a trap!

Worm—the most appropriate nickname ever—was Gestapo. And what an actor he was with those wide eyes of shock now on his traitorous face.

She backed away until her back bumped against the balcony railing. No further to go. Couldn't get away.

Monique spun and considered throwing herself off the balcony. Better that than subject herself to this man. This *Worm!*

MON DIEU! Henri felt his jaw drop and his eyes widen.

He'd thought he might never find the green-eyed, beauty of a traitor, but had sworn he would find her if it was the last thing he did. And he would kill her.

But here she was! Delivered up to him by the gods!

Stabbing a finger of accusation at him.

At him! The traitorous whore!

She backed away from him—of course, she did, the guilty snake!—and even looked like she might jump off the balcony. Of course! From fear of what he might do to her, a fear so richly deserved. Or guilt for her treachery.

Don't you dare jump and steal that pleasure from me!

Suddenly, an impossible thought struck him just as the moonlight revealed something in Squirrel's face. And at the same time, she seemed to see something in his.

Could it be?

Was it possible? Possible that she wasn't a traitor?

It contradicted every thought he'd had of her since the Gestapo broke down that door and hauled him away. Thoughts etched permanently in his brain, or so he'd thought, as one Gestapo beating after another left him bloodied and ever closer to death. Thoughts that had ignited his need for revenge against this evil beauty and then turned it into a fiery inferno. He would find her and kill her with his own hands.

But her perilous walk across the ledge made no sense if that were true. Made no sense if she were anything but what the two of them had tapped on the wall.

A PATRIOT.

He looked closer at her as she peered more closely at him, as if they could somehow discern the other's true allegiance.

The disbelief and distrust in his eyes, mirrored in hers, gave way to shocked, grudging acknowledgement that perhaps they were not enemies. *Could not* be enemies.

Were *allies. Patriots.* And would not escape without the other.

It boggled the mind.

But if true—and it had to be true—they had to hurry. Every second was precious. Any delay could mean the difference between capture and escape. And not just capture. It would be capture, endless torture, and certain death.

And that would just be the personal stakes, which paled in comparison to everything they'd been risking their lives for.

If they were caught, Alliance wouldn't find out that their secrets had been compromised. New codes and ciphers would be trusted even though they'd fallen into enemy hands. Agents at the highest levels would be revealed before they could go into hiding. Vital plans exposed for the Third Reich to see.

It might even mean the difference between winning and losing the war.

Could he really trust this woman for whom he'd felt nothing but hot, molten hatred just seconds earlier? Who he'd known with an absolute certainty was the most evil, traitorous whore of the Gestapo?

Squirrel looked like she was asking herself similar befuddling questions about him.

But they didn't really have a choice, did they? And just these few frozen seconds could prove costly.

They had to move! Now!

Henri gave a grim, determined nod and was stunned and strangely amused as Squirrel simultaneously made the same gesture. Not in acknowledgement of his, but begun at the exact same time. He felt the slightest hint of a smile cross his lips and thought he spotted the same on hers.

Time to move.

He strode toward the balcony railing, toward Squirrel. Saw her eyes flash for an instant with fear before realizing what he was doing.

He tested the strength of the railing. It felt solid. He knotted the makeshift rope of his old clothes to it, then looked down below to be sure the coast was clear.

Only darkness below.

He tossed the makeshift rope over the side, then pulled back a short length for Squirrel. They'd already covered this via Morse code, so they wasted no words. He helped her over the railing, feeling her body tense at his touch.

He understood that instinctive mistrust. Understood

it because he shared it. Could he really trust this woman? He had no choice even though their makeshift rope of knotted-together, torn clothing seemed infinitely more trustworthy.

Squirrel stood on the outside balcony edge. Then, as he held where the makeshift rope was attached to the railing as an extra precaution, she rappelled down the rope, hand over hand, until she swung onto the balcony below.

If only he could do that and still retrieve the rope.

But this combination of trousers and shirt was far too short for that. Henri pulled the makeshift rope up, untied the knot from the railing, and looped the rope in through the railing, up and back out over it until the two rope ends dangled over the side. As expected, it was several meters too short for a safe descent and easy retrieval.

He stepped over the railing with first one leg and then the other, grasped the two sides of the looped-in rope, and held them together tightly. As his pulse pounded furiously in his head, he carefully lowered himself, making sure his hands held both ropes together as if they were one. If he allowed all his weight to shift to one rope, he'd plummet to his death as the free rope rocketed up to where it was looped around the railing.

A high-wire act with no net. With about the same odds of success Squirrel had faced while traversing the ledge. But dammit, if she could defy the odds, so could he.

All for one, and one for all, popped into his head. Tapping those words now seemed like a lifetime ago, but they felt right.

All for one, and one for all.

Henri lowered himself until he neared the bottom of the two combined ropes. Still a couple meters above the balcony and with his legs dangling in the air, he began to swing like a child on a swing set.

Only this was four stories above the rock-hard pavement below.

He swung out into the cold darkness and back.

On the third swing out, he coiled his legs and on the swing back in waited until he was positioned past the railing and over the balcony. In one swift motion, he let go of one rope and yanked hard on the other.

He crashed down onto the balcony, landing hard on his left side. A second or two later, the unfurling rope dropped down onto him. Searing pain shot throughout his battered body, radiating out from his left hip and shoulder.

But he was alive! They'd gotten down to the fourth floor! The farfetched plan was working!

Squirrel rushed to his side. Bending over him, she whispered urgently, "Are you all right?"

He answered by climbing painfully to his feet. His hands a blur, he knotted the makeshift rope to the railing.

Squirrel got down to the third floor balcony uneventfully. Henri's descent was not so lucky. After swinging out over the empty air below for a third time, Henri again waited until he was over the balcony, let go of the end of one rope, and yanked hard on the other.

The maneuver had worked perfectly getting down to the fourth floor. This time, however, a knot in the makeshift rope snagged on the railing above. Instead of

Henri dropping like deadweight onto the platform with the rope furiously unfurling above him and then following him down, he swung back out over the empty air, kept from plummeting to his death only by the snagged knot. If it released before he swung back over the balcony surface, he was a dead man.

With agonizing slowness, Henri swung back to the balcony.

Close. Closer. Almost there.

And then he was just inside the railing.

Henri yanked on the rope for all his life, pistoning his legs, ready to pull the railing above down on top of them if need be. He could let go, of course, and drop to the balcony surface safely below, but without the rope they would be trapped.

Letting go was not an option. But the snagged knot would not let loose.

Until...

Squirrel darted toward him. Leaped up. Grasped fiercely onto his right ankle and yanked downward.

For the briefest instant, nothing changed except for the extra deadweight of her grunting body pulling downward.

And then...

The snag broke free!

Henri crashed down on top of Squirrel. Her slight frame cushioned his fall, but he feared he might have crushed her.

"Are you hurt?" he whispered.

She pushed him off, got onto all fours. and then unsteadily to her feet.

"*Vite!*" she whispered fiercely.

Henri retied the offending knot to make it smoother, and they made it uneventfully to the second floor, where he had assumed they would be home free. He could follow Squirrel, rappelling easily down to the ground. There would be no need to retrieve the rope. He'd simply hurl it back up to the second floor balcony so it wouldn't attract undo attention.

Except for the problem of the sentry. Invisible in the darkness from the fifth floor.

But painfully obvious now from the second floor balcony. A single streetlight in the distance illuminated two uniformed, helmeted German soldiers marching back and forth, rifles on their shoulders, in and out of the shadows on *Avenue Foch.*

Henri's heart sank. So close and yet so far.

———

MONIQUE SPOTTED the sentry the same time Worm did. A plan instantly formed in her mind. Crouching against the brick balcony wall, she whispered in his ear.

"I'll distract them so you can get away. Get word to Alliance that the documents have been compromised."

Shock covered Worm's face. "I can't just abandon you. It would be your death sentence. If one of us should die, it should be me. Just swear on your soul that nothing will stop you from notifying Alliance."

Monique smiled grimly. "I'm a woman. I've been distracting soldiers like these for years."

"Minutes ago, I thought you were a demon," Worm

said. "Now, I cannot abandon you. We got this far as a team. All for one, and one for all."

Monique reflected on how she had used a hairpin to carve those same words into a wooden panel of her cell: *All for one, and one for all.* Time to again put that principle into practice.

And so, after they quickly concocted a plan, Monique waited for the two German soldiers to march away from them toward the distant illuminated streetlight. She then rappelled to the ground, tossed the makeshift rope back up to Worm, and waited for the soldiers to turn back her way. When they did and reached the perfect position below the balcony and facing the streetlight, she emerged from the shadows.

"Forgive me, I know it's past curfew," she said in German, smiling flirtatiously. "Would either of you handsome young men have a cigarette?"

Swinging on the makeshift rope like an ape in the trees, Worm crashed into the first soldier from behind just as Monique spoke the word "cigarette." He slammed the soldier's head into the pavement, knocking him out cold.

Monique drove her knee into the other soldier's crotch. As he gasped and doubled over, she chopped the rifle out of his hands. She reversed it and slammed the butt end into his temple.

The German fell satisfyingly to the ground, knocked out cold every bit as conclusively as his comrade.

Worm blinked in surprise. They'd done it! Pulled off the longest of long shots!

"You are a tiger!" he said.

Monique grinned. "You have no idea."

THEY STROLLED through the nighttime streets to find a safe Alliance contact, Worm in a stolen Nazi uniform and Squirrel safe past curfew as his good-time girl. Along the way, they puzzled at how they'd been betrayed and concluded that the only possibility was the high-ranking Alliance member who had arranged their meeting.

So when they reached their contact and he transmitted news of the compromised documents, he added the identity of the traitor. Once the messages were confirmed—and with the camouflaged response that they had arrived none too soon and the traitor taken— Squirrel and Worm headed off in opposite directions for their next assignments, though not without first sharing a long embrace.

As they parted, they resolved that though the war might separate them, the day Paris was freed, they would meet beneath the *Arc de Triomphe* and their future together would begin.

Thank you for your interest in my books.

D H H

NEWSLETTER

Be the first to know!

If you love my writing, my newsletter is a great way to keep up with new releases, special promotions, and other content that's only available to my newsletter subscribers.

What are you waiting for?

Sign up at www.hendricksonwriter.com/newsletter-free-story/ today!

ALSO BY DAVID H. HENDRICKSON

Novels: Romance

Body Check

No Defense

Romantic Concerto for Strings and Brass

Novels: Young Adult/Sports/Historical

Cracking the Ice

Offside

Offensive Foul

Bottom of the Ninth

The Rabbit Labelle Trilogy (Omnibus)

Novels: Humor/Crime

Bubba Goes for Broke

Novels: Mystery/Suspense

Pain Train (forthcoming)

Collections

Shimmers and Laughs: Eight Wildly Hilarious Tales

Death in the Serengeti and Other Stories: Ten Tales of Crime

The Boy in the Boxers and Other Stories of Sweet Romance

Hell of a Band: Twelve Fantasy Stories

Fighting the Dying Light: Stories of Aging

ACKNOWLEDGMENTS

To Leah Cutter, Matt Buchman, Michael Bracken, Dean Wesley Smith, and Janet Hutchings, the editors who believed in these stories.

To Annie Reed, the editor and cover designer of this collection, whose expertise, advice, and friendship I can always rely on.

To my readers, whose enthusiasm helps keep me going.

To my family and friends, who support me during the valleys and celebrate with me on the mountaintops.

And above all, to Brenda, The Best Wife Ever™, for always being there and filling life's journey with such joy.

ABOUT THE AUTHOR

David H. Hendrickson's first novel, *Cracking the Ice*, was praised by *Booklist* as "a gripping account of a courageous young man rising above evil." He has since published seven additional novels, including *Offside*, which has been adopted for high school student required reading.

His short fiction has appeared in *Best American Mystery Stories 2018*, *Ellery Queen's Mystery Magazine*, *Thrill Ride - the Magazine*, *Heart's Kiss*, almost every issue of *Pulphouse Fiction Magazine* and *Mystery, Crime, and Mayhem*, as well as numerous anthologies, including over a half dozen issues of *Fiction River*. He is a multi-finalist for the Derringer Award, and his story "Death in the Serengeti" was honored with the 2018 Derringer Award for Best Long Story.

He has published eight short story collections with two more forthcoming. Currently available: *Shimmers and Laughs: Eight Wildly Hilarious Tales*; *Death in the Serengeti and Other Stories: Ten Tales of Crime*; *The Boy in the Boxers and Other Stories of Sweet Romance*; *Hell of a Band: Twelve Fantasy Stories*; *Fighting the Dying Light: Stories of Aging*; *Cape Cod Chips, Wiener Dogs, and Swiping Left: Stories of Sweet Romance*; *The Soulmate Junkie and Other Stories of Fantasy & Science Fiction*; and *Crime from Another Time: Stories of Mystery and Suspense*.

Hendrickson has published over fifteen hundred works of nonfiction, most notably his first book for writers, *How to Get Your Book into Schools and Double Your Income with Volume Sales*, and also *Travis Roy: Quadriplegia and a Life of Purpose* and *Hendu's Story: From Dream to Reality*. He has been honored with the Joe Concannon Hockey East Media Award and the Murray Kramer Scarlet Quill Award.

Visit him online at www.hendricksonwriter.com.